*S*HE stared down again at the grave. She looked and went on looking in mesmerized disbelief, but at last she raised her eyes slowly to the dark silent shadows of the trees beyond the grave, and it was then that she saw him, standing there.

Her hand went to her mouth. She took a pace backwards.

"Karen!" His eyes were wide and blank. "My God, what are you doing here?"

She tried to move, but could not. She tried to speak but the words would not come. And then he began to walk towards her.

He did not stop. He came on towards her without hesitation, his footsteps soundless on the pine-needles, and suddenly, mercifully, the power to move returned to her, and she was running blindly downhill through the dark trees, the harsh sobs jolting her body. He was running after her....

Also by Susan Howatch
Published by Fawcett Books:

THE DARK SHORE
THE WAITING SANDS
CALL IN THE NIGHT
THE SHROUDED WALLS
THE DEVIL ON LAMMAS NIGHT
PENMARRIC
CASHELMARA
THE RICH ARE DIFFERENT
SINS OF THE FATHERS
THE WHEEL OF FORTUNE
GLITTERING IMAGES
GLAMOROUS POWERS
ULTIMATE PRIZES
SCANDALOUS RISKS

April's Grave

A NOVEL BY

Susan Howatch

FAWCETT CREST ● NEW YORK

A Fawcett Crest Book
Published by Ballantine Books
Copyright © 1973 by Susan Howatch

Library of Congress Catalog Card Number: 73-88401

ISBN 0-449-20994-6

This edition published by arrangement with Stein and Day Publishers

Two-in-one volume Main Selection of the Bargain Book Club

Printed in Canada

First Fawcett Crest Edition: December 1975
First Ballantine Books Edition: December 1983
Ninth Printing: July 1992

April's Grave

One

One

1

Marney had not thought about the Conway twins for a long time. He knew that Karen, the elder twin, was working in New York and that she had neither sought a divorce from his friend Neville nor even acknowledged Neville's maintenance payments by so much as a Christmas card, but Karen had seemed remote, part of a buried past which had no relation at all to the present, and it had never occurred to Marney until he was standing by the window of his hotel room and staring out over Central Park that Karen was the only person he knew in the entire city.

He had just concluded a successful working-holiday, lecturing at five Canadian universities, and had visited a friend at Harvard before flying south to New York. He was booked to sail back to England the next day, but meanwhile he was faced with an evening in Manhattan and was beginning to wish he had stayed overnight in Boston instead. He could have caught an early shuttle flight and still have had plenty of time to reach the docks and board the liner in comfort. Boston would at least have been cooler. Beyond the window and the labored hum of the air-conditioner, the Park shimmered in the heat-haze of a summer evening. Even the trees, Marney noticed with professional interest, were beginning to look as burnt as the worn, parched grass.

Marney always noticed trees. Trees were his business. Sometimes it seemed to him that the world of trees and natural vegetation was a world preferable to the scrabbling ant-heaps of humanity in which he was forced to live and work daily. Marney did not like cities, did not like New York. America had always made him uneasy. It was just as he was trying to imagine what it could be like to live and work in New York that he thought of Karen.

He thought of her twin sister April Conway almost simultaneously but so immediate was his rejection of the memory that the thought was little more than a brief tremor of the muscles, a small shallow breath, a flicker of some nebulous emotion in the furthest recesses of his mind. He turned aside and picked up the phone by the bed.

"May I help you?" said a voice a moment later.

When he had obtained Room Service he ordered a whisky, and then, remembering that he was a foreigner using incorrect vocabulary in a foreign language, he amended the order to a scotch on the rocks. Really, he thought, America was very exhausting. He sat down on the edge of the bed, an Englishman a long way from home, and thought of the solitary peace of his flat by the river at St. George's Square, the mellow comfort of his office near Birdcage Walk, the pub where he and Neville would go for a sandwich at lunchtime . . . It was three years now since Karen had left Neville and returned to America. She had written to Neville's lawyers to inform them of her address and give instructions that maintenance payments were not necessary as she had returned to her former job on the staff of one of the huge magazines dedicated to the young career woman. Neville had made the alimony payments just the same. Neville would, thought Marney. It would be intolerable for Neville to realize that Karen could exist independently of him and that he could give her nothing whatsoever, not even money. He would rather pay her the unwanted money than face the fact that there was no longer anything she required of him.

The waiter arrived with the scotch.

Later, after he had finished the drink, Marney stood up restlessly and went back to the window to look at the trees. He supposed he should have dinner. The Americans, he knew, dined early, but unfortunately his stomach, trained as it was on English eating habits, was not hungry. He decided to order another drink.

He meditated for a long time over his second scotch and wondered what he should do. He knew all the signs by this time and was far too intelligent not to admit his state of mind to himself. If he stayed in the room much longer he would remain there the whole evening and get very drunk. He always got drunk when he thought of the Conway twins. He must go out, he told himself, go out, find a good restaurant, perhaps meet a charming companion . . . The scotch was already making him unrealistic. He was in his forties, but looked older and had none of Neville's dark good looks or tailored elegance. "Charming companions," such as he envisaged them, were not acquired in the course of a single evening by the crook of a little finger.

He suddenly realized that he was appallingly lonely. On the strength of this realization he ordered another drink, and then in a moment of panic at his weakness he fumbled with the Manhattan telephone directory by his bedside and began to search among the columns for Karen's phone number.

He could not find it, and then as his third scotch arrived and he began to sip it, he wondered if Karen had reverted to her maiden name on returning to New York. He began to search through the Conways, and suddenly he saw her name and the eastside address in the seventies. He stood staring at her name for a moment while his memories clouded his mind and sought to overwhelm him, and presently he found he was not thinking of the Conway twins at all, but of his own friend, Karen's estranged husband, Neville Bennett.

He thought of Neville for a long time.

At last he picked up the receiver and asked the reception desk to dial Karen's number.

The line began to ring, and he listened to the loud long buzz, so different from the soft purr of an English phone. It rang three times before she picked up the receiver, and he heard again the low attractive voice he remembered so well. Her voice was exactly the same as April's, the only identical feature shared by unidentical twins.

"Hello?"

"Karen?" He pronounced her name with the long

English "a", the pronunciation she had used in England, and knew at once from her sharp intake of breath that he had already given himself away. "Karen, this is Marney."

There was a short absolute silence. Then she said slowly: "Marney!" but he could not tell whether she was pleased or sorry.

He heard himself stammer some explanation about his lecture tour and how he was sailing back to England on the next day. "I—I was wondering . . . Just on the off-chance, of course—well, are you doing anything tonight? I thought perhaps we might have dinner . . . Of course, I realize it's very short notice, but—"

"No," she said. "I'm not doing anything tonight."

"Then—perhaps—" He could feel himself reddening as he spoke. "Would you care to have dinner with me?"

"That would be very nice," she said, her voice still charming, but as carefully expressionless as the cliches she selected to accept his invitation. "Thank you."

"I'll call for you at your flat, then," he said, and conscientiously correcting himself added: "Your apartment, I mean. Would it be too soon if I came in half an hour's time?"

"No, I can be ready by then." He heard a slight change in her voice and caught his first glimpse of her astonishment at the unexpectedness of his call. "This—this is such a surprise, Marney, please forgive me if I sound a little dazed. How is everyone in England?"

"Oh, fine." He was sure she was going to ask about Neville. He was so sure that when her question came it took him by surprise.

"How's April?" she said.

There was a silence.

The phone would have slipped in his clammy hands but he was holding the receiver so tightly that his knuckles hurt.

"April?" he said after a long while.

"Isn't she still in England?"

"April?" he said. "In England?" He tried to pull himself together. "You mean she isn't back in America?"

There was a pause. Then: "I haven't seen her since the day I left Neville," Karen said. "I assumed she had stayed on in England."

"We all thought she'd gone back to America."

"You mean no one's seen her or heard of her for the past three years?"

"Haven't you?"

"No, of course not! I guessed——" She stopped. Then: "But that's extraordinary, Marney! Where on earth can she be?"

And it was only then, more than three years after her disappearance, that it was first realized April Conway was missing.

2

Karen had been trying not to think about her twin sister April since the day she had decided to try not to think of Neville Bennett any more. Now, as she replaced the receiver after speaking to Marney, she discovered that her memories of both of them were scarcely less painful even now after three years. The realization was so vivid and so unpleasant that for a long moment she merely remained exactly where she was in the still room, but at last she left the couch and went to look for a cigarette.

Of course, she had thought of April from time to time and had never been foolish enough to suppose that she would not. One could not simply forget a sister, let alone a twin sister. But she had made up her mind that she had no wish to see her again. She had left April in England; let her stay there, she had thought at the time. What did it matter? She was past caring what April did and wanted only to get away, to try to pick up the threads of her old life which she had abandoned so readily when she had first met Neville Bennett.

But she would not think of Neville. Not just yet. It was painful enough to think of April, to think and remember . . .

She found a cigarette, lit it, and tried to focus her thoughts on the present. She must be ready when Marney arrived in half an hour's time. It was kind of him to have called. Marney had always been kind. In the old days she had been rather fond of him.

Moving quickly into her bedroom, she selected an outfit to wear for the evening, shed her working clothes, and took off her make-up to reapply it afresh. There really wasn't much time. She worked quickly and deftly, and the concentration on the familiar motions helped to still her confused thoughts. In the end she was ready on time and Marney was late, so she lit another cigarette and in spite of all her will-power, allowed herself to think of Neville.

Neville Bennett. She could still remember her amused astonishment when they had met for the first time. There had been a party in a chic apartment near Washington Square; a friend of hers had married a lecturer at the University. "Darling," the friend had screeched to her above the roar of the cocktails, "a wonderful man . . . *must* meet him . . . English professor—botanical science, darling—devoted to trees . . . *so* sweet . . ." And Karen had turned, expecting to see a whitehaired, stooping scholar, and had come face to face with all six feet of the charm and grace and frank sexual interest which emanated from Neville Bennett.

He was thirty-eight and a widower. His wife had died in a road accident two years earlier shortly after the birth of their son, and because Neville seldom referred to her, Karen had assumed that it still hurt him to be reminded of his loss. In fact, as she discovered later, his silence stemmed not from grief but from guilt. He had become bored with his shy, quiet, self-effacing wife whom he had married in the belief that an attraction of opposites was likely to prove long-lasting, and although he had done his best to conceal his boredom he had found it increasingly difficult to do so. He had, it was true, made great efforts to be a satisfactory husband, and to some extent he had been rewarded for his efforts when his son was born; somewhat to his surprise he had been fascinated by the baby, so intrigued by its newness and helplessness that he had automatically responded with more warmth towards its mother, but before he had had the chance to attempt a new beginning with his wife she had been knocked down while crossing a London street and had died before reaching hospital. This abrupt termination of his marriage was distressing enough, but what was even more distressing was that he now felt guiltier than ever about his secret boredom before the arrival of the baby. It was as if fate had deprived him of the opportunity to turn over a new leaf and had left him instead with a handful of useless good intentions. As the months passed, he spoke about his wife less and less until, by the time he had met Karen, he so seldom mentioned his marriage that for a long while she had thought he was a bachelor.

He had certainly behaved like a bachelor. It had not taken her long to realize that Neville was enjoying his new life as a single man so much by then that to persuade him to change his status a second time would be very difficult. However, she was sufficiently mature to know how to play her cards correctly and at last, after many anxious moments, several exasperating delays, and more than one occasion when she had wished they had never met, she flew to England for the wedding.

They were married in London at the Savoy Chapel, and Marney was best man. Neville's unmarried sister Leonie, who had been keeping house for him in Cambridge since his first wife's death, welcomed Karen politely, and the child, who was still little more than a baby, accepted her with enthusiasm. As for April, she hadn't even bothered to send a telegram. She was still in Hollywood at that time, still concentrating on being photographed at premieres and dating "useful" people. The only member of Karen's family who had been present at the wedding had been Karen's brother Thomas, then living in Paris. Thomas was considered the black sheep of the family by his brothers who had all settled down on Minnesota farms and married local girls; he spent his time seeing the world and working as an actor or film extra to finance his travels.

I wonder, thought Karen, as she waited for Marney

that evening, whether Thomas has heard from April during the last three years. It was unlikely, since both April and Thomas had long been in the habit of disappearing for long stretches of time, and neither of them were in touch with the family in Minnesota, let alone with each other, but it was still possible. Since they were both on the fringes of show business, Thomas might have heard some whisper of gossip on the grapevine.

By chance she had his current address. He had sent her a birthday card a week ago from Rome.

"Filming a hokum epic here," he had scribbled. "They've dug up a bible story again. What would scriptwriters do without that book? I've got a part in an orgy scene, Sodom-and-Gomorrah style. I have to sprawl on a couch, toy with a leg of chicken and leer at an Italian slave-girl. Very good pay, and the slave-girl's not bad either. I'll be here till the 20th—mail me a line or two if you get the chance."

Thomas had never liked Neville. She remembered Thomas's arrival in England for the wedding and his first meeting with his new brother-in-law.

"Rather a rolling stone," said Neville afterwards. His voice was carefully devoid of contempt, but she knew nonetheless that he was contemptuous. Neville, who had been a success all his life, had no patience with people who were by his standards failures.

"Kind of a smooth operator," said Thomas to her in private. He tooks pains to sound casual and unconcerned, so that there was no risk of her taking offense. "More like a business tycoon than a professor. Are you happy?"

Half-annoyed, she assured him that she was. Neville

had, by this time, left academic life and had begun working for the government in London. He had bought a beautiful house at Richmond and Karen had been busy both with her new home and with her small stepson who was then two-and-a-half years old. The child was still very small and it was easy to believe that at birth he had been so minute that his father had described him as being no bigger than a pinch of snuff. The comment had not been forgotten; even after his christening the nickname had lingered on.

It was just after Snuff's fourth birthday when April had come to England. Karen had already been worrying about her marriage for some months, but had managed to convince herself that she was worrying unnecessarily; although it had certainly seemed to her that Neville was now taking greater pleasure than usual in talking to attractive women at the parties they went to, she told herself that her imagination was too vivid and it was foolish to suspect when there was no cause for suspicion. And then, suddenly, April had arrived, and her suspicions had grown to such monstrous proportions that finally there had been nothing else left to do but to prove the suspicions justified.

"The bitch!" Thomas had commented with his customary frankness, but not everyone had held the same views on the subject. Neville, for example, had liked April at once; she was a suitably admiring audience, and Neville, like most men, loved to be admired. Marney had been reserved and withdrawn; April's unabashed femininity had made him shy, although Karen had suspected at the time that he admired April more than he cared to admit. Neville's sister Leonie had been frankly disapproving. Within a short time, Karen had

begun to realize dimly that her relationship with her
husband was deteriorating much more rapidly than before.

The buzzer rang in the kitchen. Recalled with a
painful wrench to the present, she went to answer it
and heard the doorman say from the lobby: "A Dr.
West is here to see you, ma'am."

"Tell him to come up."

She had not seen Marney since before she had left
Neville. She wondered how much he had changed.

The doorbell rang and, after glancing at herself
quickly in the mirror, she went to open the door.

He was there, looking just the same. And it was the
sight of Marney which made all her old longing for
Neville surge within her again, and she realized with
mingled horror and hopelessness that she still loved
him.

3

They dined at the Tower Suite and went on afterwards
to the Plaza for drinks. They had talked of Neville, of
Neville's sister Leonie, of the child. Leonie was apparently acting again as Neville's housekeeper as well
as looking after Snuff. "Neville's taken a lease on a
carriage house, very charming, off Kensington High
Street." They had talked of Marney's work, reminding
each other of the coincidence which had led years ago
to himself and Neville working in an advisory capacity
for the same government-owned concern. "I still have
affiliations with the Varsity and often wish I'd never
left teaching, but Neville's in his element. He's better in

this job than he was with the students." They talked of Karen's job, of New York and London, of current events, of other people they knew, and finally when there was no one and nothing else left to talk about, Karen said:

"It's very odd about April."

It seemed almost as if he had been waiting for her to introduce the subject; she saw his features relax and guessed he was glad she had spoken of April again without reticence.

"Haven't your parents heard anything of her during the past three years?"

"I'm sure they haven't heard a word. I've been back every year for Thanksgiving and April was never mentioned. She hurt them a lot, you know, by voluntarily cutting herself off from them. And my brothers—the ones who live in Minnesota—never mentioned her."

"What about your brother Thomas?"

"I thought I would write and ask him if he's heard anything. There's just a possibility that he may have some idea where she is."

"Haven't you asked him before if he knew where she was?"

"I haven't seen him since the business with April three years ago, and he's a bad correspondent. I've spoken to him a couple of times on the phone, but each time it was long-distance and we didn't have time to do more than confirm that neither of us had any sensational news of her. I knew the affair with Neville had come to nothing because Neville wrote and told me it was finished, but I didn't know where she'd gone afterwards. To be honest I didn't want to know. I didn't even want to talk about her with Thomas."

There was a pause. Marney took another sip of his Benedictine.

Karen said casually: "Neville mentioned in his letter that she didn't stay at the farm long after I left."

He did not look at her. "She left the same day."

"Was Neville much upset?"

"I think Neville had had quite enough by that time," said Marney soberly. "When he found her clothes were gone from the farm and that she had walked out, I think he was more relieved than sorry."

Karen was aware of bewilderment. "But when did she leave?"

"No one was quite sure. I suppose it must have been some time while you were lost and Neville was searching for you. April would have been alone at the farm then, if you remember." He paused delicately. "After Neville left the farm to look for you, April must have packed her bags, rowed across the lake and thumbed a lift from a passing car. One of the two boats was found on the other side of the lake afterwards, so that would seem to confirm the theory."

Karen was silent. She had no wish to recall the past, but against her will she was remembering each event which had led up to the ultimate disaster; she saw again April in London, April flirting with Neville at the house in Richmond, her brother Thomas arriving unexpectedly from abroad and trying to warn her what was happening—as if she were blind and could not see it for herself! Poor Thomas, he had been so upset. Then had come the discovery that April's plane ticket for a weekend in Paris was in fact a train reservation to Scotland where Neville had important business in the Highlands. She remembered how she had followed

April north a few hours later, and how, unknown to her, Thomas had done the same thing, remembered their meeting at the little hotel at Kildoun, the tortuous journey in the hired rowing boat across the lake to the small farm where Neville stayed whenever he was in Scotland on business. He had been there with April. The shock of that confrontation had been so great, despite the fact that she had known what she was going to find, that Karen had barely paused to speak to them. She had rushed out over the moors, not knowing or caring where she was going, until eventually she had lost herself in the forestry plantation, in the dark silent acres of Plantation Q, and when Neville had found her three hours later she had insisted on being taken to the foresters' lodge where she had phoned Thomas in Kildoun and asked him to come at once to take her away. He came; they left together, and after that she had never seen either Neville or April again.

"I'm sorry," Marney was saying awkwardly, "perhaps we should talk about something else."

"No, I don't mind talking about it now after all this time." She lit a cigarette with a steady hand. "I was just puzzled that April had left the farm—and Neville—so suddenly and vanished into the blue. It seems odd somehow, unlike her."

"Well, now you come to mention it," said Marney, "I suppose it was. But at the time I don't think it occurred to any of us that there was a mystery involved. We were all too glad to be rid of her, and were too upset by all that had taken place. I suppose that's why we merely accepted her departure and didn't stop to question it in any way."

"Yes, yes, I can understand that. I guess Neville hasn't heard any word from her since?"

He hesitated. "I doubt it."

She wondered for a moment to what extent Neville would have confided in him.

It had always seemed odd to her that Neville and Marney were such friends. Marney had appeared to her to be a typical bachelor, ascetic, scholarly and self-contained, whereas Neville . . .

"I'm surprised Neville hasn't wanted to get a divorce and remarry," she heard herself say before she could stop herself, and then immediately regretted the remark. The champagne at dinner followed by the liqueurs seemed to have loosened her tongue.

"Really?" said Marney. "One might almost say the same thing about you, my dear." And she was just realizing with relief that the liquor had made him even less reserved than she was when he added: "Why haven't you married again? A woman like you ought to be married. Didn't you ever think of getting a divorce from Neville?"

"Yes, I thought of it."

"And decided to stay married to him?"

"There was no one else I wanted to marry. And I couldn't face the prospect of putting the divorce wheels in motion."

"Hope you're not still in love with him," said Marney, finishing his Benedictine. She saw now that he was much more inebriated than she had supposed earlier. "Women always fall for Neville. It's such a mistake. At least he's fond of the child. That's something, I suppose. I'm glad he's fond of the child."

"Yes, Neville was devoted to Snuff—and so was I!"

She sighed. "How I'd love to see Snuff again! I've thought of him so often."

"I'm sure you have." He hesitated before adding: "Another drink?"

"No, really, Marney, no more. It's been a lovely evening, and I've enjoyed seeing you again."

He saw her back to her apartment. She half-wondered if she should ask him in for coffee, but he solved the problem for her by taking her hand in his and thanking her for making the evening so successful. "I hope I'll see you again one day before too long," he said, and much to her astonishment leant over and kissed her clumsily on the cheek. "Goodbye, Karen. God bless you."

And he was gone, his footsteps receding towards the elevator, and she was left alone in the solitude of her apartment.

She undressed, went to bed, and lay awake for a long while. At length when it became patently obvious to her that sleep was out of the question, she got up and wrote two letters, the first to her brother Thomas in Rome, and the second to her friend and former room-mate Melissa Fleming who now lived in London. She wanted to ask Melissa if she could stay with her during any possible future visit to England.

4

Melissa Fleming was English but had worked in New York for two years and had met Karen there before Karen had met Neville. The two of them had shared an apartment in the Gramercy Park area for a year; they had not been close friends, but Karen was the kind of person who could get on well with nearly everyone, and Melissa, who needed a room-mate for economic reasons, was quick to realize that Karen was one of the few women whom she might just possibly be able to live with. On the whole, Melissa did not find her own sex congenial companions. As Karen was then a stranger to New York she knew few people; she was prepared to like Melissa and Melissa was prepared to like her. The friendship proceeded cautiously for several months while both of them continued to lead their separate lives as far as possible, and only began to founder when Neville arrived on the scene and Melissa realized that Karen attracted him more than she did.

Melissa prided herself on her sex-appeal: the idea of playing second fiddle to Karen was definitely not appealing.

However, before the friendship dissolved amidst the destructive atmosphere of jealousy, first Neville and then Karen left for England and Melissa resigned herself to the fact that Neville was completely out of her reach. Having been salvaged so unexpectedly, the friendship flourished again by letter as Melissa remained in New York and Karen settled down as Neville's wife four thousand miles away. Later Melissa inherited a sizeable legacy which induced her to return to England and start up a business there, but by that time Karen had left Neville and had returned to America so that the width of the Atlantic Ocean still lay between them. Gradually their letters to one another became more infrequent and their friendship more nominal. In the end Melissa, immersed in her new business, no longer bothered to write.

Melissa was a designer. She had worked in fashion houses, had some flair and a considerable amount of business acumen. The providential legacy was used to open a boutique off Knightsbridge, and because Melissa was prepared to cultivate the right people and had certain valuable contacts dating from the days when she had been to the right schools, she soon had the right clientele. The boutique had been highly successful now for nearly two years and Melissa lived above the shop in a modern, sophisticated and expensive flat.

She was not married. Her one and only venture into matrimony had been an adolescent mistake and she preferred not to talk about it.

When the letter from Karen came, she was first conscious of a slight feeling of guilt because she had not written to Karen for many months and had more or less decided to lose touch with her. After all, thought Melissa practically, one couldn't keep in touch with *everybody;* besides, Karen seemed to belong to the past now, and Melissa was much too interested in the present and the future to have time for sentimental memories.

She opened the letter and was conscious of a shock. It had never crossed her mind that Karen would come back to London to see the child, and yet, Melissa had to admit, it was a perfectly logical thing to do. Karen had always been exceptionally fond of her small stepson, particularly since she had had no child of her own.

She glanced back at the letter. Karen was frank in asking if she could stay at the flat. That could be very

awkward. Well, perhaps awkward was too strong a
word, but the stiuation might possibly prove embarrassing.

Still frowning slightly, Melissa picked up the white
telephone receiver and began to make a call to Neville
Bennett with whom she happened, at that moment, to
be having an affair.

5

Leonie Bennett, who now acted as Neville's housekeeper, was only two years older than her brother but
looked and behaved as if she were very much the elder
sister entrusted with a brother who needed all the care
and attention she could give him. Her parents had left
her a large amount of money at their deaths, so she had
never had to work for a living but had instead passed
her time either by zealously pursuing her favorite outdoor activities, gardening and golf, or else playing endless rubbers of bridge at the club to which she belonged
in London. Except for the eighteen months during
which Neville had been married to Karen, she had been
obliged to look after her nephew since soon after his
arrival in the world, and this had resulted in the
number of her social activities being reduced. However,
the acquisition of a Swiss nanny while the child was
still very young had helped the situation, and now that
he was at school she was once more free to do as she
pleased. As for the house, she enjoyed running it and
gained great pleasure from looking after her brother as
lavishly as possible, but she did miss having a garden;
window boxes were a poor substitute and nothing in-

teresting would flourish in the little backyard of the
carriage house, although she had tried several times to
grow roses in tubs. But in spite of this disadvantage she
was content. She was very fond of her brother, and no
doubt it was because of Neville that Leonie had become so fond of the child, for she had never been
greatly interested in children before and had certainly
never shared Karen's absorption in Neville's son.

She was reminded of Karen with an unexpected jolt
when not merely one but two American letters appeared on the mat after Neville had left for the office
that morning. The mail had been arriving progressively
later all that week and she had just returned to the
house from taking Snuff to school when the mailman
pushed the letters through the front-door slat on to the
floor below.

She went to pick them up and saw the American
stamps at once.

One letter was for Neville, the other for the child.

Leonie paused, consumed with curiousity. She knew
very well that Karen had not written to Neville since
leaving him three years ago. What would she be writing
about now? Leanie seriously debated whether to steam
Neville's letter open and then reseal it, but finally decided against this idea as she felt sure Neville would
somehow find her out. Neville was so clever. After
simmering with curiousity for another unbearable half
hour, she had a brainwave. The child would never
know. She would open the letter to Snuff.

Five minutes later, the letter in her hand, she was
dialing the number of Neville's office with trembling
fingers.

6

The child attended school at a French Lycée near his home and had been there just long enough to have a confused but increasing grasp of the French language. He had already decided that the nickname Snuff was the kind of adult absurdity that would make his life difficult among other children, and had rechristened himself with an extravagantly French name which he had learnt from his former Swiss nanny. He did not like to use his own name, which was Neville. Neville was a special name with special connotations, much too sacred for his own everyday use.

That afternoon his Aunt Leonie met him after school as usual and took him home under her personal supervision. He was already beginning to regard this as yet another embarrassing example of adult absurdity, but experience had taught him that his aunt was easily upset and he knew better than to provoke a new emotional crisis.

"Good afternoon, Aunt," he said politely as they met outside the school, and remembered to smile. If he did not smile she would assume he was unhappy and would start to worry about him.

Aunt worried about everything. Given half a chance she would worry if there was nothing to worry about.

"Snuff darling . . ." To his profound distaste she even embraced him within sight of his schoolfriends. He disentangled himself very firmly and hoped no one had noticed.

Aunt was tall, too tall for a woman, and rather thin

with no curves, and had a dark bony face with teeth and a nose.

"Darling, I've got some very unexpected news for you. You mustn't be too worried or upset. It's really very exciting." Her voice was a shade higher than usual; he looked at her with extreme suspicion.

"It's about your step-mother—about Aunt Karen."

"Oh yes?"

She was twisting her gloves nervously. "You know she went abroad three years ago."

"Yes, of course. She's living in New York." He looked at her with astonishment. Surely she remembered that Aunt Karen wrote to him and sent him beautiful presents on his birthday and at Christmas? For a long time now he had been able to read the letters all by himself.

Aunt said in a rush: "She's just written a letter to Daddy—and there's a letter for you as well which I opened ready to read to you as soon as you came home." And then as Snuff opened his mouth to protest that he liked to open all his letters himself, she said rapidly: "She's going to come and stay in London for a while."

The news was so surprising that he even forgot to be angry. "Really?" he said with interest. "You mean Aunt Karen's coming to London soon?"

"She wants to see you again, darling."

Snuff failed to see anything odd about this. "Does Daddy know yet that she's coming to London? Did he get the letter yet?"

"I telephoned him at the office but he was out. I had to leave a message."

"With Uncle Marney?"

Aunt looked taken-aback. She often telephoned the office and asked to speak to Neville even when she knew Neville wasn't there. Snuff had noticed this long before he started school, but he supposed Aunt had not realized he had noticed. He always wondered why she didn't ask for Marney directly if she wanted to talk to him so much.

"Well, that's all right, isn't it?" he said defensively. "Uncle Marney will give Daddy the message."

"Oh yes," said Aunt. She sounded a little absent-minded. "Marney will tell him."

7

Neville had had a long business lunch at the Athenaeum with a Scottish land-owner interested in forestry techniques. By the time he returned to his office it was nearly three o'clock. As he had been out most of the morning he was not altogether surprised at the long list of telephone calls which had accumulated since his departure.

"Your sister called twice," said his secretary. "The first time I switched her to Dr. West's office and the second time she just left a message for you to phone her. Dr. West also wanted to speak to you, by the way. Then Miss Fleming called twice, first this morning and then again just now . . ."

Melissa. He wondered what she wanted. He hoped she did not intend to be difficult or create undignified feminine scenes. He was gradually easing himself out of

his relationship with her, and with great tact and a
large amount of diplomatic skill was stealthily cutting
each of the emotional bonds which had once linked
them together. She had appeared to accept this so un-
demurringly that he had assumed the wish to terminate
their affair was mutual, but it was hard to be entirely
sure; perhaps it was safer to assume that she would
enjoy an emotional scene if the opportunity for one
arose.

"Get Marney for me, would you?" he said absent-
mindedly to his secretary. He would leave the chore of
answering Melissa's calls till later. Taking off his raincoat, he shook the water from his umbrella into the elegant Adam fireplace and adjusted his dark tie in the
old-fashioned Victorian mirror.

Vanity, thought his secretary.

"Dr. West? One moment, please, I have Professor
Bennett for you."

Neville took the receiver from her. "Thanks . . .
Marney?"

The room was still and peaceful, the silence broken
only by the rain slewing against the pane and blurring
the view into St. James's Park. His secretary was moving out of the room. The door closed softly behind her
but he did not hear it.

Suddenly he did not even hear the rain on the window any more. His eyes still watched the trees swaying
in the park beyond, but he did not see them. He was in
another land altogether, in another time long ago, and
there were lamps glowing in a room of a small Highland farm and long shadows veiling a face he thought

he would never see again, and outside the sky was still
light with the afterglow and the lake had the opaque,
mysterious quality of darkened glass.

"I'll talk to you later, Marney. I see a call's come
through on my other line."

He slammed down the receiver and held it there for
a long moment. Then with great deliberation he put on
his raincoat again, picked up his umbrella and walked
out of his office without even telling his secretary that
he would not be back that day.

8

In a hotel in Rome not far from the Via Veneto, a letter with an American stamp was handed to the young
American actor who was staying there. Letters from
home were a rare luxury for Thomas Conway. He put
it in his pocket, strolled to the nearest outdoor cafe and
then at a table bathed in sunshine and with his cup of
capuccino before him he opened the envelope and read
the letter inside. Ten minutes later he was back in his
hotel and writing a reply.

*Thanks for the letter. It was good hearing from you
again—too bad I didn't understand a word you said! What's
all this about April? I couldn't make you out at all. Do I
think something's happened to her, you say? Sure I think
something's happened to her! She's Sheik Whoosis' nine
hundredth wife or she's entertaining sailors in Rio de Jan-
eiro or she's decorating some fancy whorehouse in Bel-Air.
So who cares? I wish to God you'd quit worrying about her
and let her take her own primrose path to wherever she
wants to go. You say it sounds as if she treated Neville bad-*

ly. *Good! It was about time someone did. I think it's a
great idea for you to make a trip to Europe to see the kid,
and with any luck I can fix things so that I'll be in England
to see you. Be sure and let me know when you plan to come.
Incidentally, I don't know whether you're planning on a
reconciliation with Neville, but I wouldn't get too sold on
that idea, if I were you. It's none of my business, of course,
but all I can say is that any man who leaves you for a
flirtation with April deserves all he gets, and I wouldn't
like to think that all he gets includes a reconciliation. You
look after yourself and don't get taken for a ride by a lot of
smooth talk, or what the English so politely call charm.
And stop worrying about that sister of ours. What does it
matter if no one's seen her for three years? I haven't noticed anyone weeping and beating their breasts in lamenta-
tion.*

Seeya!
LOVE, THOMAS

Two

1

When Neville left the office he walked through St. James's Park to Buckingham Palace and then across the Mall and through Green Park to Piccadilly. The rain had stopped and the evening was not unpleasant; St. James's Park was a mass of summer blooms, and the beauty of the lush grass and thick-leaved trees soothed his mind and made him feel more relaxed. He reached the Ritz, drank two double whiskies and felt almost normal. Finally he found a cab and within a quarter of an hour was unlocking the front door of his house in Adam and Eve Mews.

The letter with the American stamp lay waiting for him on the hall table.

Leonie came out of the kitchen. "Neville—"

"Yes, yes, there's a letter from Karen. I saw it." He

knew he sounded irritable, but this was not unusual as he found his sister an irritating woman and had long ago decided not to feel guilty about it. If it had not been for the child he would never have consented to her acting as his housekeeper, but he wanted more than anything for Snuff to have some semblance of a normal home even though Neville had—by his own stupidity—deprived him of Karen.

"Snuff took the news very well," Leonie was saying. "Very well indeed."

"Why shouldn't he?" He escaped into the drawing-room, his fingers tearing the envelope apart. "Forgive me if I sound abrupt, but I've had a tiresome sort of day."

"Oh, of course, dear—I quite understand."

"Is dinner ready?"

That got rid of her. She went into the kitchen, and he closed the drawing-room door and opened out the sheet of thin airmail paper.

Dear Neville,
I've decided to take my vacation in Europe this year and hope to spend a few days in London with Melissa. My flight is booked for the 18th, and I'm looking forward to the chance of seeing Snuff again. I'll be in touch with you when I arrive.
KAREN

He stood there, not feeling bitter or angry or unhappy, but merely conscious of disappointment. Finally he tore the letter into tiny fragments, and to be certain that Leonie would not be able to piece them together, he set a match to them in the ash-tray.

He was just watching them burn when the telephone rang.

He picked up the receiver. "Hello?"

"Neville—"

Melissa. His mouth felt dry suddenly.

"Melissa, I can't talk to you now. I'll phone you back later."

He put down the receiver and turned away in relief but the phone immediately rang again. He grabbed the receiver in exasperation.

"Look, Melissa—"

"Must you," she said coldly, "be quite so childish?"

He would have hung up on her but he could never endure to suffer criticism and then deprive himself of the chance to answer back.

"It's not a question of being childish!" he said, much irritated. "I'm sorry I was so short with you just now, but—"

"Short!" she said. "Short! I'd call it by a much stronger word than that! I think it's about time you realized, Neville, that I—"

He sighed. He saw the pattern then, the remorseless inevitability of conciliation, pleading, flattering and finally succeeding, and felt jaded. Not so long ago he had found her attractive, a passable attempt to replace someone irreplaceable, but now all magic was gone and his interest was dwindling into indifference.

"I'm absolutely sick and tired of the way you treat me at times—I've often wondered if I mean anything to you at all."

He had heard it all before. He did not even bother to smother a yawn, but then his boredom drifted into a shaft of pain as he remembered Karen. How could he ever have looked upon Melissa as a replacement for her? He must have been demented. Anyone less suited to replace Karen would have been hard to imagine.

"Thank God you were never in a position to marry me!" she was saying. "At least I was spared that mistake."

He had heard that before too. It meant that somewhere and at some time during the course of their relationship, Melissa had secretly hoped for marriage even though she had always protested just the opposite.

"I don't recall that I ever proposed to you," he said very coolly.

"You often hinted you would get a divorce—"

"Well, I did think about it—"

"—and that when you were free—"

"I never said anything of the kind."

"You implied—"

"You chose to read an implication into my remarks."

She called him a name and hung up.

He shrugged. She would ring back in half an hour. She always did. Even having a lover who infuriated her was better than having no lover at all.

He thought of Karen again. The memory was so clear then that he winced with the pain of it. "I wish I hadn't married you," she had said. "You're clearly unsuited for marriage." And she had gone. He had thought at once, carelessly, not worrying too much: she'll come back. She's bound to come back. She'll calm down and realize that even having an erring husband is better than having no husband at all.

But she had not come back. She had walked on a plane to America and he had never seen her again.

He had a vivid memory then of the horror of it all, the shame of having to admit he had treated his beautiful charming wife so badly that she even refused to have any communication with him, the demoralizing embarrassment of failure in his private life, and worst of all the pain, the emotions he had never experienced or anticipated, the dreadful nagging ache of loss. How he had missed her! He could not sleep, eat, or work for the pain. He was desolate and miserable. It was brought home to him then with shaming clarity that he had never ever known what love was until he had suddenly found himself without the one he loved. In the end he had swallowed his pride—he, Neville Bennett, who had never had to humble himself to any woman! —and written to her, begging her to come home. It had taken him six hours and five drafts to complete, and alhtough he still wasn't satisfied with it he had sent it off and waited hopefully for an encouraging response.

She had never replied.

He had tried to harden himself then, attempted to adjust. He had lost her and made a mess of his personal life—and hers—but it would be foolish and unrealistic to go on hoping for a miracle that would never happen. He had decided to reorganize his life and bring about such changes that there would be as little as possible to remind him of the past. He sold the house at Richmond where they had lived since he had resigned his teaching position and begun to work for the government on forestry projects. He did not want to live at Richmond any more. Instead he had taken a lease of the house in Adam and Eve Mews, made arrangements with Leonie for her to renew her role as housekeeper,

tried to meet other women to take his mind off what
had happened . . .

And all the time there was the child, asking why
Karen had gone, asking when she would be coming
back, reminding Neville of how much he had lost despite all his futile efforts to forget.

The door opened.

"Daddy?" It was Snuff's bed-time and he was in py-
jamas, his face scrubbed, his hair standing up in front
in an aggressive tuft. "Aunt Karen wrote a letter specially for me even though it's not Christmas or my
birthday." He waved a grubby scrap of paper. "She's
coming next week and she'll take me to the zoo and
Madame Tussaud's and buy me a bicycle at Harrods—"

"May I see?"

The child handed it over, beaming up at him happily. "Isn't it nice?"

Darling Snuff,
I'm going to come and see you very soon, the Wednesday
after you receive this letter, and I'm so looking forward to
seeing you again that I can hardly wait to fly across to Lon-
don. Be sure and think of all the places you'd like to go and
visit—I remember you told me in that letter which Aunt
helped you write last Christmas that you like the zoo and
Madame Tussaud's, so maybe we could go there again, if
you wanted to. Do you still want that cycle? If you do we
can go to Harrods or some other store together and you
can choose the one you like best. Longing to see you,
darling, lots of love . . .

"Isn't it nice?" repeated the child, still beaming up at
him.

Neville made an effort. "Very nice!" He smiled at his son and patted the child on the head. "I didn't know you wanted a bicycle. Why didn't you tell me? I'd have taken you to Harrods myself and bought you the best bicycle in London if I'd known."

After pondering the diplomatic reply to this, Snuff suggested that Neville and Karen could both go to Harrods to choose him the best bicycle. "Because then it would be twice as good," he explained, "since it would be a present from two people instead of one. Would you go to Harrods with Aunt Karen, Daddy?"

"Perhaps. Yes, if you like." He smiled at Snuff again, but his thoughts were already wandering back to his marriage and he was conscious, as he had been conscious so often before, of that insidious sense of failure. The memory of his recent quarrel with Melissa added to his depression. As Snuff trailed off to bed Neville had a longing to see Marney, his friend of a quarter of a century, the one person who was always the same and who never changed. They had met as freshmen at Cambridge when they were eighteen and even though Neville had always outshone his friend socially and academically they had still remained friends.

Leonie called from the dining-room that dinner was on the table.

It was a pity, thought Neville as he went into the other room, that Leonie had not married Marney, but then Marney had always regarded women so warily that it was not surprising that he had remained a bachelor. Marney had seen straight through April from the beginning. Neville could remember him saying: "Leave her alone, let her be, she's not for you—Karen's worth ten Aprils—a hundred." Marney had made every effort to turn Neville's interest away from April, but Neville hadn't listened.

"I suppose Karen wants to come back to you," said Leonie tight-lipped over the roast beef and Yorkshire pudding. "I suppose she's had enough of living alone."

"I doubt it." He saw she was already worrying about the possibility of being usurped. If the usurper had been Neville's well-bred, very English first wife then no doubt Leonie would have relinquished her prized position in the household with grudging good grace, but the idea of being usurped by Karen would be most upsetting. Leonie, always distrustful of foreigners, had never fully accepted Karen as part of the family, and had never fully recovered from her original belief that Karen was a pretty adventuress who had skillfully and shamelessly manipulated Neville to the altar.

"Well, I suppose we should be grateful that she's bothering to come and see Snuff," she observed acidly. "He was so upset when she left, poor lamb. I always thought it was disgraceful the way she went off to America without considering the child's feelings in any way."

"He isn't her child."

"Yes, but she behaved toward him as if she were his mother!" Leonie had bitter memories of how Snuff had turned from her and accepted Karen with such ease. "She confused him, poor child. It wasn't fair."

"I'm sure the hardest part of her decision to leave England three years ago," said Neville deliberately, "was the fact that she had to say goodbye to Snuff. But once she had made up her mind to leave me she had no choice but to leave him, too. She had no claim on him. She couldn't take him with her."

"I should think not indeed!" Leonie exclaimed, and with an unmistakeable edge to her voice she added: "You're always so ready to stand up for her—you're too generous in forgiving, Neville. After all, when it all boils down to it, what happened? She left you on the spur of the moment, abandoned all her responsibilities and caused you endless embarrassment among your friends. I always did say that Americans were much less scrupulous about the marriage ties than we are. And I'm sure they're more immoral than we are too, and much more prone to affairs."

The memory of the episode with April and its disastrous conclusion jerked instantly back into Neville's mind against his will; without warning he seemed to hear April's voice once more, the words which she had spoken during that last terrible weekend when she had followed him to Scotland, to the farm and Plantation Q.

"Poor Karen!" she had said mockingly after Karen had discovered them together and stumbled blindly out of the farm to escape from her discovery. "What a shock for her to find out she can't be lucky all the time. Why, Neville, where are you going? What are you doing? Oh Neville, please—don't go after her! Leave her alone— it serves her right! Why should you run after her when you don't care about her any more?" And when he had said nothing she had rushed at him in a frenzy of rage and shouted that she wouldn't let him leave, that she was pleased his marriage was finished, glad that Karen had lost him. "Glad!" she had screamed at him. "Glad, do you hear? Glad!" He could hear her voice still, ringing in his ears, shrieking through his nightmares. "I'm glad . . . glad . . . GLAD!"

He felt ice-cold suddenly. His body shivered.

Leonie was just about to continue her dissertation on Americans when the telephone rang again and Neville escaped in relief to answer it.

"Neville, I'm sorry I was so bitchy earlier—"

It was Melissa, just as he had anticipated. She was exactly the same as so many other women. Karen was the one who was different.

2

When Karen arrived in London it was late at night and she felt tired after the long tedious hours in the plane. The journey through the Customs and Immigration Department seemed agonisingly slow. At last when she was free to leave, she found a cab, gave the driver Melissa's address in Knightsbridge, and sank back thankfully against the ancient leather upholstery.

She was back.

Her mind had been so filled with thoughts of Neville and the child during the past few days that now when she was at last within a few miles of them she was unable to think of them at all. She was aware of a curious numbness muffling all poignancy and longing and rendering her detached, almost careless. I'm back, she kept telling herself. I'm back. But the thought was difficult to assimilate, for the new road into Central London was as modern as any American freeway and the darkness hid the English green of the countryside from her eyes. And then surprisingly quickly the countryside was gone and the suburbs began and there were signboards with English names so that her presence in this

foreign land seemed at last to be a reality. Acton,
Shepherd's Bush, Hammersmith, Richmond . . .

Richmond was where she had lived with Neville
after he had left Cambridge and had begun to work for
the government in London. Richmond was just a few
miles away across the Thames. I'm back, she thought
again, I'm back. And the past came rushing up to meet
her, almost drowning her in wave after wave of memory, but the memories were happy and she strained to
grasp each one and savor it again. She realized to her
surprise that in America she had tended to remember
only her unhappiness, but now, here in London, the
unhappiness seemed as remote and as far away as
Scotland and that terrible weekend when she had followed Neville and April north to Plantation Q.

Her mind closed automatically, obliterating the train
of thought before it reached the memory of her sister at
Neville's in Scotland. That was all over, closed; she
was back in London and remembering happier times,
and if the memories were tinged with sadness because
they belonged to the past they were also tinged with
excitement because she was closer now to the past than
she had been for three yeras.

The cab reached the entrance of Melissa's flat. The
cabbie took her suitcases up to the front door, and
suddenly there was Melissa, very smart in that same
cool indolent way which men found so attractive, and
beyond Melissa were soft lights and comfort and the
end of the journey.

"Why, Melissa, you haven't changed at all!"

"Darling, how devastating! You mean to say I haven't even improved slightly during the last few years?"

The cabbie was waiting to be paid, and the English

money confused her unexpectedly so that she gave him a bigger tip than she had intended. Three years of handling cents and dollars had blurred her memory of pounds, shilling, and pence.

"You must be quite exhausted," Melissa was saying. "Let me make you some coffee."

"Well . . ." Melissa's spare room was small but elegant. There were flowers on the dressing-table, English roses, and a couple of fashion magazines placed unobtrusively near the bed. Karen abandoned her suitcases without unpacking them and within five minutes was relaxing on the living-room couch while Melissa brought in the coffee.

"I really appreciate you having me to stay like this," she said to Melissa presently. "I thought of staying at a hotel, but—"

"Darling, what on earth for? It's lovely to see you again! Now tell me all about New York and your job and all the poeple I used to know."

Time passed. Both cups of coffee were filled, emptied and replenished more than once. Finally Melissa gathered together the coffee cups and turned to take them out to the kitchen. Then: "What are your plans for tomorrow?" Karen heard her say casually.

"I expect I'll go shopping in the morning and call Leonie to find out if I can see Snuff after he finishes school in the afternoon. Apparently his term doesn't end till the day after tomorrow so I won't be able to see him tomorrow morning. I guess I shall have to phone Neville and make arrangements with him."

"You're not expecting any difficulty about getting Neville's permission to see the child?"

"Oh no, Neville wrote back in reply to my letter and

said I could see Snuff whenever I wished—Neville's not vindictive, and besides I've been in touch with Snuff ever since I left. It's not as if I were returning to him as a stranger whom he had already forgotten."

"Hm-hm." Melissa was in the kitchen. "You're not looking forward to seeing Neville again?"

"Not particularly." She was amazed at how colorless her voice sounded when her heart was bumping so uncomfortably and her hands were tightly clasped with tension.

"I was wondering if you were hoping for a reconciliation."

"I came to see Snuff, not Neville."

"I see. Yes, of course." Melissa was rinsing the cups and saucers under the tap.

"Have you seen anything of Neville recently, Melissa?"

The tap was turned off. There was a slight pause. Then: "Well, as a matter of fact, darling, yes. Rather a lot." She was moving around in the kitchen; Karen heard her open a cupboard door and close it. "After you left we became quite friendly. Well, not *directly* after you left. Perhaps a year or two afterwards. Over the past twelve months or so I've been seeing him frequently."

There was another puase. Karen, the first wave of shock subsiding, was aware of mounting tension. Her limbs began to ache unbearably.

"Actually, darling, you came back just at the right moment. I've been trying to break off with Neville tactfully for some time, but . . . well, you know Neville! It's all been rather awkward really. I was so glad when I heard you were coming back because I hoped—well,

I hoped Neville would be diverted, if you see what I mean . . ."

Karen tried to speak but could not. Amidst all her confused emotions she was conscious first of anger for letting herself imagine Neville would have spent the past three years in celibacy to mourn her departure, then of anger that she should care how he had spent the past three years, and finally of anger that she should feel angry. Whatever happened she must not let Melissa see that she cared in any way for Neville or was hurt by what Melissa had just told her. That would be too humiliating. Besides it was obviously all as embarrassing for Melissa as it was for her.

". . . never any question of marriage, of course," Melissa was saying carelessly. "Neville never even thought of getting a divorce. He just used to come here now and again."

There was an ache in Karen's throat suddenly, tears in her eyes. She turned, pulled back the curtain, forced herself to stare out at the London skyline beyond, and tried not to think of Melissa here with Neville, Melissa eating, drinking, sleeping with Neville, laughing with him, enjoying life, savoring his nearness to the full . . .

"Honestly, darling, it was nothing much really. We had a holiday once in Italy, a couple of weekends in Paris, but it didn't *mean* anything. How could it? You know Neville."

The words were like knives, tearing and wrenching the fabric of happy memories Karen had woven for herself since her arrival in England. Pain blinded her eyes, drummed in her ears.

"I wouldn't have done it, of course, if I hadn't taken for granted that you were going to divorce him. I held

out against him for the longest time, and then, well, I
thought, 'Karen never writes to him, obviously he
means nothing to her any more. Perhaps she's even
found someone else.' And I did find him attractive.
And charming. And . . . well, darling, you know."

Karen did know. She stared out into the darkness
and in her mind she was picturing Neville as she had
last seen him in Scotland, and wondering if she would
ever be able to endure seeing him again.

"Darling, I hope I haven't upset you," Melissa was
saying from the doorway. "I wouldn't have told you,
but really I've nothing to hide and from my point of
view the affair is quite finished so I thought it best to
make a clean breast of it before someone else told you
out of spite. I'm sure Leonie will manage to drop a hint
or two when you see her tomorrow. Poor woman, she's
so—well, *soured*. Rather sad really. Neville told me
she's still secretly in love with Marney. Talking of
Marney, I suppose when you met him in New York he
didn't mention that Neville and I—"

"No, he didn't say a word about it."

"Dear Marney—always such a gentleman! But I
should imagine he knew what was going on—he and
Neville are such close friends."

Marney had warned against a reconciliation, Karen
thought. Perhaps he had spoken with Melissa's involve-
ment with Neville in mind.

"Now," said Melissa, abandoning her vague, ab-
stracted tone and changing the subject briskly, "are you
quite sure you have everything you want in your room?
A glass of water, perhaps—"

Karen assured her that there was nothing else she needed.

"Then I'll say goodnight," said Melissa, turning to open the door of her own bedroom. "I do hope you sleep well. Oh incidentally, I knew there was something I was meaning to ask you! Did you manage to find out what had happened to April? You told me you were writing to Thomas—"

"Thomas knew nothing and neither did my family in Minnesota."

"How extraordinary! Then she really has disappeared?"

"I guess so. If she hadn't been in the habit of disappearing for long spells at a time maybe we'd have realized it sooner, but I was the only one she kept in touch with, and after that time in Scotland . . . well, I wasn't surprised not to hear from her afterwards." Karen was wondering as she spoke why Melissa should be so interested in April. "However, Thomas wrote and said he would try to get to London to meet me, so that was good news. I hope he makes it—I haven't seen him for such a long time."

"Of course, he went to Scotland with you when April and Neville—"

"Yes," said Karen, "he did. Goodnight, Melissa, and many thanks."

But it wasn't until she was leaning back against the spare room door and letting the tears stain her cheeks that she asked herself in irony why she should thank Melissa for making her so unhappy.

3

She managed to sleep for about five hours and woke the next morning feeling less tired but still depressed. Pulling herself together with an effort she had a bath and dressed with care before going into the kitchen to make herself some coffee and toast. Melissa had already gone downstairs to the boutique after telling Karen to make herself at home and eat whatever she liked from the refrigerator and pantry. The morning papers lay on the kitchen table, the first "Telegraph" and "Express" that Karen had seen for years. She read them leisurely in an attempt to keep her mind from dwelling on her conversation with Melissa the previous evening, and then at last when she was too tense and nervous to sit still any longer she went over to the phone to call Leonie.

The conversation proved easier than Karen had anticipated; Leonie, formal but polite, told her that Snuff finished school at three-thirty that afternoon. Perhaps Karen would like to take him out to tea at four? Karen had, of course, spoken with Neville. She hadn't? Well, in that case . . . Leonie sounded faintly scandalized.

"I'm going to phone Neville now," said Karen. "But if you don't hear from me again, I'll see you at four this afternoon at your house. Thank you, Leonie."

She put down the receiver in relief and then, suddenly feeling unequal to the task of phoning Neville at that moment, she found her handbag and moved impulsively out of the house into Knightsbridge. At Harrods she bought a woolly giraffe and a snakes-and-ladders set for Snuff and lingered longingly among the fur coats before eating a snack lunch and returning to Melissa's flat. Back in her room, she paused. Melissa was out, lunching with a client, and Karen was alone. She had been shopping. There was no more unpacking left to do. The time had come when she could no longer put off making the phone call to Neville, but even as she realized this, she decided to have a cup of coffee and put off the moment a little longer. Just as she went into the kitchen the phone began to ring.

She picked it up cautiously. "Hello?"

A pause, very slight. Her scalp tingled in a flash of comprehension. "Hello?" she said again rapidly. "Who's this, please?"

"How are you, Karen?" said Neville, his voice very smooth and charming. If it had not been for that small pause she would have thought his manner completely effortless. "Welcome back to England. Snuff's much looking forward to seeing you."

"I was just about to call you." Her fingers were gripping the receiver so tightly that they hurt. She was vaguely amazed at how cool and composed she sounded. "I spoke to Leonie this morning and we thought that perhaps I might call for Snuff at four and take him out to tea. I hope that's all right with you."

"Yes, of course. His school breaks up tomorrow for the summer holidays, you know, so you'll have plenty of time to see him after that."

"Yes, you mentioned that in your letter." Neville's acknowledgment of Karen's letter had been as brief as her announcement of her visit.

There was another small pause.

"How long will you be here for?" said Neville presently.

"Between two or three weeks, I think. I've got a tentative reservation for the fifth."

"I see."

"How's Marney?"

"Marney? Oh, well enough, I think. Well, look, Karen, I won't hold you up now as I'm sure you're very busy, but I hope all goes well this afternoon—I shan't be home by four, of course, but Leonie will be there and I know Snuff is impatient to see you . . . I'll be in touch with you."

"Fine," said Karen. "Thank you, Neville."

She put down the receiver with trembling fingers and reached for a cigarette. The flame ignited, flared, died as she struck a match and blew it out. After a while she began to wonder what he was doing, what his reaction had been. Had he too reached for a cigarette and lit it unsteadily? Or had he stared out across Birdcage Walk to St. James's Park just as she was now staring across the roofs of Knightsbridge? Probably not. Probably he had merely summoned his secretary and dictated a memo on Plantation Q, or busied himself in writing some report. Or perhaps he had strolled down the corridor to Marney's office to tell Marney casually that he had just spoken to Karen. What did it matter anyway? Surely what mattered was that she was left with her dread enhanced at the thought of meeting him again. If his voice could succeed in shattering her composure so completely it was certain that his presence would reduce her to new emotional depths which she had no wish to experience. It would be foolish to betray that she still cared in any way for Neville when there was no future in caring. To Neville she would seem merely part of the past; he would be more interested in Melissa than in her.

Turning very slowly she went to her room to rest for a while before it was time for her to leave Knightsbridge and set out for Adam and Eve Mews.

4

The child was excited. He skipped along the pavements and danced around each tree planted by the roadside, and all the world was as bright to him as the afternoon sunshine. His Aunt Leonie, who had collected him from school, followed at a more sedate pace, her lips pursed with misgivings as she thought of the meeting to come. As usual she was worrying. What effect would this have on the child? Was he suffering even now from the separation of his father and step-mother? Would he suffer in the future? Would it be better if Karen had never come? But Karen was here in London and would soon be at the house. The meeting was unavoidable now.

Snuff knew his aunt was worried, but as she was always worrying about something he was not concerned. He danced down the steps and when he saw his stepmother waiting by the front door he danced right up to her and into her arms. She was exactly as he remembered her, and he thought with delight how nice she looked and how pleasant she smelt and how prettily she spoke English. He had specially remembered her accent. "I knew you'd come back one day!" he said with

shining eyes, and began to wonder idly if she had
brought him a present.

The woolly giraffe was a great success. Snuff knew
he was really too old for soft toys, and had to pretend
not to like it as much as he did, but secretly he was
very pleased. The game looked promising too. He
looked at his step-mother with renewed interest and
wondered if she would buy him "dame blanche" for
tea.

"What's that?" she said later when they were in the
tea shop, and he discovered with amazement that she
knew no French. He had thought everyone all over the
world learnt French, particularly French food names
like "dame blanche" which was white ice cream with
hot chocolate sauce. A few minutes later, covered with
chocolate sauce from ear to ear, he scraped his spoon
furiously against the bottom of the cup so that not a
drop should be wasted, and told her all about his life at
his French Lycée.

She listened and ordered him another "dame
blanche." It was then that he first realized what a good
time he was having, and he wondered vaguely if she
would come to England more often. She was much
more "sympathique" than Aunt Leonie.

"Why do you live in America?" he asked presently.

She seemed to take a long time answering. In the
end she said: "It's my country—where I was born and
brought up. I work there."

"But you lived here once."

"Yes."

He was dimly aware of feeling confused. "Because
you were married to Daddy?"

"Yes."

He felt he wanted to ask questions, but he could not put the questions into words. He was only aware of shadowy puzzles in his mind, of bewilderment which it was beyond his power to express.

"Will you live here again one day?"

"Perhaps."

Her eyes were watching her plate. He could only see her long black lashes. He glanced at her plate too, but there was nothing there.

"With Daddy?"

"I don't know."

He groped in his mind for words. "Doesn't he like you?"

She glanced up at him then and he saw to his horror that her eyes were brilliant with tears. Every muscle in his body went rigid. He pushed back his chair. "Can we go now?"

She nodded without speaking, fumbling in her purse for change. Moving very quickly he slid past her and edged his way through the shop to the door. While she paid the bill at the cash desk he stared through the glass and watched a policeman directing the traffic.

They went outside together.

"I guess it's time for us to go home," she said, and she sounded so calm and composed that he stole a glance at her. Her eyes were quite dry too, he noticed with relief. He felt himself relax a little. "Your aunt will be wondering what's happened to you."

She stretched out her arm to take his hand in hers but he pretended he didn't see it and skipped on ahead through the rush-hour crowds, careful never to be out of her sight but equally careful not to be near enough to enable her to talk to him. He had enjoyed his tea with her, but now he had had enough and wanted to go home. Her air of mystery frightened him and he was afraid to talk to her again at that time for fear she might tell him what terrible secret had brought the tears to her eyes. He was afraid of the unknown, yet afraid of knowing too much, and in all his confusion he only knew that he must not mention his father to her again.

They reached the house and Snuff stood on tiptoe to ring the doorbell. His step-mother was lingering behind, he noticed puzzled, and he wondered if she was frightened; she was carrying her gloves and twisting them over and over again between her fingers.

"Honey, I think I'd better say goodbye now—I'll come and see you again tomorrow . . ." Her voice trailed off as the door opened, and she stood very still, her eyes looking straight over his head to the doorway beyond.

The child swing round.

"Hello Snuff," said his father. "I deduce from your faint chocolate moustache that someone has been indulging you in 'dame blanche' again. Did you enjoy your tea?"

Snuff opened his mouth but closed it uncertainly as he saw that his father was already looking past him to the woman beyond. And as the child watched, an onlooker at a scene he did not understand, he saw his father smile slowly and hold out his hand as if he were offering her something which was both mystical and yet real.

"Won't you come in for a moment, Karen?" said Neville Bennett to his wife.

5

They dined at Quaglinos and Neville ordered a bottle of her favorite vintage white Burgundy to go with the Dover sole she chose from the menu. First they had chilled cucumber soup and freshly-baked soft rolls, and then after the entrees, Karen chose the sherry trifle while Neville selected baked Alaska. The coffee, when it came, was strong and aromatic and flavorful. Neville ordered two glasses of Grand Marnier to accompany it, and then offered her a cigarette.

"How are you feeling?"

She smiled at him. "Still dazed, I think!" She looked very composed, he noticed, but not relaxed. He himself felt better now. The wine had lulled his tension and brought a genuine relaxation to him, but he still felt oddly vulnerable. He wanted her very much. Three years had changed nothing, least of all her power to attract him, and he wondered with a vague feeling of incredulity how he could ever have looked at another woman. The memory of April seemed like some nightmare, remote and unreal and even a little fantastic. As for Melissa, he had completely forgotten her. Melissa had ceased to exist, even as a memory. In fact his memory was capable of recalling nothing at that moment save for his past with Karen, just as his mind was capable of focusing on nothing except the immediate present and his pleasure in being with her.

"Well," he said. "We seemed to have talked a great deal about a great many subjects, but there's still a certain amount left unspoken."

"Sometimes it's better to leave things unspoken."

"Sometimes," he said, "but not always." The waiter brought the liqueurs and departed. Neville took a sip from his glass and the Grand Marnier caressed his palate with its distinctive flavor. "About April, for example," he said deliberately, not looking at her. "We have to mention her name sooner or later or else it will continue to lie between us like some monstrous skeleton in the cupboard. You must know that I regard the incident with April as one of the most foolish, contemptible things I've ever done. If I could somehow obliterate the incident from my past I would do so at once, but of course that's not possible, so I just try to obliterate it from my mind. I treated you very badly, I know. If I hadn't met April—"

"If you hadn't met April, it would have been someone else," said Karen, her voice cool and dispassionate. "You wanted an affair, Neville. Since we're being so frank with one another, perhaps I can remind you of how you began to behave at parties, how often you used to hurt me even before April came to London—"

"All right," he said, "I'll admit it. I admitted it in that letter I wrote to you and I'll admit it again now. I treated you badly and behaved even worse—but I didn't realize how much I loved you until you were gone, Karen, and by that time it was too late to make amends. As far as April was concerned, at least I wasn't wholly to blame. I made no rendezvous with her, you know; our meeting at the farm wasn't pre-arranged. I went there on business and she chased after me as soon as she heard you weren't going to be there. I know that when you arrived and found us together you thought you could see exactly what was going on, but it wasn't as you supposed. You didn't know that Leonie was on holiday at the farm at the time—that April had misjudged the situation and that I wasn't alone after all—"

"Yes, you explained in your letter."

"I admit that if Leonie hadn't been there—"

"Yes."

"But there was no rendezvous. I had no part in bringing April there—it was her fault she was there, and her fault alone. Don't put all the blame on me and forget April altogether."

"I hadn't forgotten April and I never shall." She ground out her cigarette. "Have you heard from her since?"

"Not a word. After you—discovered us together that morning I quarreled with her and rushed out after you. That left April alone at the farm, since Leonie had left earlier to walk over to the foresters' lodge at Plantation Q to see Marney. By the time I eventually got back several hours had passed and April had gone. I looked around, saw her clothes and suitcases had vanished and then discovered that one of the boats was gone from the jetty. So she must have packed after I ran out after you, rowed herself across the lake and managed to get a lift from a passing car."

"But how odd that she should have left so suddenly!"

"I don't think so. We'd quarreled. I'd told her to go." He took a gulp of liqueur and fidgeted with his glass. "She must have left soon after I did," he repeated. "Leonie came back from the lodge at about eleven, she told me later, and April wasn't there then. I'm not sure what time I left to look for you but it must have been around nine-thirty. So some time between half-past nine and eleven o'clock that morning—"

"April disappeared into the blue."

"Well, if you want to put it that way, yes. I suppose she did. More coffee?"

"Please."

"Frankly I was too upset to think much about it at the time. I was only too glad to be rid of her."

"You had quarreled with her finally, then?"

"Irrevocably." He was still fidgeting with his glass. "She—but it's much too unpleasant to talk about in detail. Let's just say that she suddenly showed her true colors to me during the quarrel, and I was horrified. You knew—realized—" He hesitated unexpectedly.

"What?"

"She was—unbalanced. You must have known that."

"Isn't that rather a strong word? She had her problems, certainly, but—"

He laughed. "What an American way of putting it!" Then, serious again: "You always used to defend her, didn't you? You were always prepared to make excuses for her, and now I see you still are. Why's that, I wonder?"

"I—I don't know. I've never been sure—it's hard to explain—"

"It sounds as if you too have your problems!"

"Haven't we all!"

They laughed. Neville, sensing that the moment was propitious, tightened his grip on his liqueur glass.

"Karen, I didn't mention it to you before but I'm supposed to be going to Scotland to Plantation Q on business on Monday. I could put it off to spend more time with you and Snuff in London, but I don't want to do that. I want you to come with me to Scotland and we can have a week by ourselves at the farm and give ourselves a second honeymoon. Won't you come? I want you back more than anything I've ever wanted in all my life. I know you'll be reluctant to go back to the farm and Plantation Q, but I'm a great believer in facing unpleasant memories and not letting them haunt you, and there are no ghosts there, Karen, I know for I've been back often. It's still the beautiful secluded place it always was, and it would take more than April's viciousness to destroy its beauty and its peace. Come and see for yourself. I can promise you I'd be a damned sight better husband to you this time than I ever was before—I've learnt my lesson and I've learnt it in a way I'll never forget. I love you and that's the truth, I promise. I love you a thousand times more deeply than I ever did before."

Her hand moved involuntarily. He was aware of her beautiful fingers, of the rings he had given her nearly five years ago, and he glanced up searchingly into her face, but her lashes veiled her eyes and her expression was hidden from him. He waited in an agony of suspense, every nerve strained for her response, and still she did not answer. In the end he said desperately: "I know it must be hard for you to trust me after the way I treated you—"

And she said, interrupting him: "That's true certainly, but there are other factors which make me hesitate."

"Such as?" The liqueur glass slipped in his hot palm; a drop of Grand Marnier scarred the white cloth. "Look," he heard himself say with a clumsiness which was foreign to him. "I haven't been faithful to you during the past three years. I think you know me better than to suppose that I could be celibate for that length of time, and besides, when you didn't reply to my letter I decided it would be better to try and forget you—"

"You needn't makes excuses," she said. "I understand."

The sweat was prickling at the back of his collar. His mouth was dry. "I had an affair with Melissa," he said. "Perhaps she told you—yes, I can see she did! That's typical! I suppose you were wondering when and if I was going to mention her. Well, there's little to say except that she was my mistress on and off for about a year and that I started to lose interest in her about three months ago after rather a disastrous weekend in Paris when she became much too emotional and dramatic for my peace of mind. As far as I'm concerned the affair is finished and was finished even before you wrote to tell me you were coming to England. I never loved her, but there were times when I enjoyed her company and felt reasonably fond of her. You'll notice that I use the past tense. At the moment I find her more irritating than anything else."

There was a silence. Around them the restaurant was alive with a low turmoil of sound; the hum of conversation, the ring of cutlery, the dull clink of plates.

"I see," said Karen.

"I suppose Melissa painted the situation a little differently."

"A little."

"She's bound to make some sort of scene if she believes there's a chance of our being reconciled. I'd advise you not to confide in her and pretend there's no question of a reconciliation."

"Uh-huh." She was fingering her rings.

He leant forward. "What are you thinking, Karen?"

She raised her eyes to his. He felt his heart turn over and the longing ache in his throat because she was so beautiful. He wondered if she could tell from his expression how much he wanted her.

"It's very difficult," she said at last. "I shall have to think it over for a while."

"Yes," he said automatically, his reflexes masking his disappointment and anguish. "Yes, of course." So much for his plans for them to spend the night together at the Dorchester. He had thought in such detail about his first night with her for three years that the realization that it was to be postponed was indeed a bitter pill to swallow. "Perhaps we can have dinner again tomorrow?" he said levelly. "What are your plans?"

"Snuff finishes school at noon and I wanted to take him out to lunch and then to the zoo or Madame Tussaud's. I had no plans for the evening."

"Then you'll dine with me?"

"I'd love to." She smiled at him, and the blood seemed to tingle through his veins.

He took a taxi with her to Knightsbridge but stopped some way from Melissa's apartment in order to avoid any risk of Melissa witnessing their parting. There was an unlighted shop window, a darkened doorway, and he drew her into the shadows to kiss her as he had dreamed of kissing her all through the evening. She felt light in his arms, but that was probably because there was so much strength in him, for her hands were firm enough as they clasped behind his neck, and her mouth was hard and passionate beneath his own.

"The hell with you 'thinking it over,' " he said unevenly at last. "The hell with that. Let's get a taxi—there'll be a room at the Dorchester—"

But she was withdrawing, elusive as ever, and her face was shadowed and hidden from him by the darkness. "I must think," he heard her say, her voice low and indistinct. "Please, Neville. Give me a chance to think it over." And then even as he shrugged his shoulders in a gesture of resignation she had turned aside from him and was walking away down Knightsbridge to the door of Melissa's apartment.

6

"Darling," said Melissa, rising to her feet with a smooth fluent motion of her body. "I hardly expected you back tonight! What happened? Did something go wrong?"

The last thing Karen wanted to do at that moment was to talk to Melissa. "Nothing happened," she said shortly, retreating to her bedroom. "We had dinner and talked for a while. What were you expecting to happen? I'd told you that I had no intentions of a reconciliation."

"Oh, I know you had no intentions, but you know Neville." She was in the doorway, poised and unashamedly curious. "Didn't he suggest—"

"I thought Neville's business was no longer yours,

Melissa," Karen interrupted, and then added hastily: "I'm sorry, I don't mean to be rude, but—"

"Darling, of course not! I understand. I was only wondering, that's all. I'm glad you had a nice evening." But still she hovered in the doorway.

"As it happens," said Karen, "Neville's due to go to Plantation Q on Monday, so I doubt if I'll see much more of him on my trip."

"Really?" Melissa's voice was sharp. "Well, it's just as well you don't want a reconciliation, isn't it, or he might suggest taking you back there! I should think that must be the last place on earth you would want to go to."

Karen said, unthinking: "He said there were no ghosts there—" And then nearly bit off her tongue as she realized she had given away the fact that Neville had spoken of a return to Scotland together.

But to her amazement, Melissa did not seem to notice. "So he said there were no ghosts, did he?" she murmured. "I wonder." And she turned and moved indolently back into the living-room.

Karen followed her. "What do you mean?"

"Oh nothing." She lit a cigarette and shook out the light with a languid flick of the wrist. Then: "Karen, what do *you* think happened to April?"

Karen stared. "Why, I don't know! I guess she's found some man somewhere, and . . . well, what do you think happened to her?"

"Oh Lord!" said Melissa. "How should I know? I wasn't at Plantation Q on the day she—disappeared. I've just listened to various people reminiscing—how can I judge? It merely occurred to me how strange it was that she apparently vanished so suddenly into thin air."

"The general opinion seems to be that she rowed herself across the lake and hitched a ride to—"

"But darling!" said Melissa deprecatingly, "imagine it! I've been to the farm—I stayed there for a week last summer actually, while Neville had business on the plantation—and quite frankly I just can't see a girl like April rowing across the lake to the road. Hell, darling, that's a long way to row! *I* certainly couldn't have done it! A tough, sporty spinster like Leonie—well, yes. I can see her making light of it, but a fragile slip of a girl like April who couldn't have had any rowing experience since her childhood by the Minnesota lakes—"

"Then how else could she have got away from the farm?"

"Well, that's just it, darling," said Melissa. "I rather wonder if she ever did get away."

Three

1

"That's preposterous!" said Neville furiously. "Quite preposterous! I hardly thought Melissa would stoop so low, even if she were jealous of you, but it's clear she has no scruples at all."

He was dining with Karen again the following evening. Earlier in the day Karen had taken an enthralled Snuff to the zoo and to Madame Tussaud's and had then met Neville at eight. Now an hour later she had hesitantly told him of Melissa's theory that April had met her death by accident, and was in spite of herself astonished at the violence of his reaction.

"It's too much!" he added enraged. "That, I swear it, is the last night you stay under her roof! I'll not have you stay with her a moment longer—it's obvious that she's full of malice and jealousy and is determined to pay me back for terminating the affair—"

"But Neville," said Karen, half-amused by his vehemence, half-bewildered by the force of his anger, "anyone would think that Melissa suggested you murdered April! All she suggested was—"

"She suggested to you that April never left the farm, didn't she?"

"Yes, but—"

"If April had had an accident—suppose, for example, that she had fallen in the lake—how would that account for the fact that her suitcases disappeared with her? Besides, corpses resulting from accidental death seldom disappear without trace. They don't bury themselves—or tie weights to their limbs so that they stay on the floor of a lake. If April met her death by accident, then where's her body? Why hasn't it been discovered? There's nothing whatsoever to suggest that April had an accident and never left the farm—or the lake."

"That's what I said to Melissa, but she merely shrugged her shoulders and said she thought it was all very suspicious."

"The devil she did! She was trying to make you think I'd killed her, that's all! She's so damned eager to prevent a reconciliation between us that she decided to try to tell you I murdered your sister—"

"Don't you think," said Karen, "that that's just a little too melodramatic?" She was certainly not going to admit that she had lain awake half the night wondering if Melissa had meant to do this and whether it was at all possible that April might somehow have met her death three years ago in Scotland. The possibility of an accident did seem unlikely, particularly since no body had been discovered. But if she had not died by accident . . .

"Melissa *is* melodramatic," said Neville. "It's just the kind of trick she would employ to try to make sure you don't agree to a reconciliation."

"But Neville, she must know I would never believe you killed April—"

"Precisely," he said. "Because April was never killed in the first place. Only it pleases Melissa for reasons of her own to invent this monstrous story—"

"Well, she never actually said—"

"She implied it, though! My God, I can see through her even if you can't! The trouble with you, my dearest, is that you simply won't hear a word against anyone, even your worst enemies—in fact you take great pains to speak up in their defense even after they've stabbed you in the back! But I see through Melissa all right, and I'm damned if I'll let you go back to her flat either tonight or any other night. You can stay at the house, if you like—we haven't a spare bedroom, but I can easily sleep on the sofa in the livingroom. And since I'm off to Scotland on Monday it'll only be for a couple of days anyway."

There was a silence. The waiter flitted past and paused long enough to refill their coffee cups.

"If you prefer," said Neville, "I would pay for a hotel for you."

"I—" She hesitated, not knowing what to do. The thought of staying on at Melissa's was certainly distasteful, but the thought of staying under Leonie's critical eye was little better.

"I think you should move to a hotel," said Neville,

making up her mind for her. He glanced at his watch. "I'll come with you back to Melissa's, collect your luggage, and then take you to the Dorchester."

She knew quite well what would happen at the Dorchester. She paused, toying with her cup, her eyes watching the steaming black coffee, and suddenly she was remembering a thousand small things, the stiff pace of her job in New York, the loneliness of her Manhattan apartment, the men for whom she cared nothing, the meaninglessness of her life beneath the rush and confusion of her daily living. And it seemed to her suddenly that for three years she had been living in shadow and here at last was another chance to walk back into the light.

She looked up at Neville. He was very still, but she saw how his knuckles gleamed white as he rested his hand on the table, noticed the strained set to his mouth.

"Well?" he said lightly. "What do you say? Do you think that's the best thing to do in the circumstances?"

Still she hesitated. Then finally after a long while she heard herself say: "Yes . . . yes, I think it is. Thank you, Neville."

2

Mercifully, Melissa was not at home when they returned to pick up Karen's luggage. Karen spent a full ten minutes trying to write her a note while Neville casually helped himself to a whisky and soda in the living-room, but the ultimate result of her attempts seemed worse than inadequate; however, the circumstances were so awkward that any attempt at a written explanation would inevitably be fraught with difficulties. In the end she wrote: "It seems I underestimated the possibility of a reconciliation! I shall probably be going up to Plantation Q with Neville on Monday and will give you a call before I go—if you should want to contact me I'll be at the Dorchester through Sunday. Meanwhile many thanks again for your hospitality and please excuse this sudden departure."

Leaving the note propped up on Melissa's dressing-table, she went back into the living-room.

"All right?" said Neville abruptly.

She nodded. "I hope so."

"Then let's go."

Karen could hardly wait to leave the apartment. It occurred to her how embarrassing it would be if Melissa arrived home at that moment, but fortunately their departure was without incident. Karen gave a sigh of relief. She had no wish to see her friend's face when Melissa read the note and learned of the pending reconciliation.

The Dorchester was aglow with soft lights, the epitome of peace and comfort and luxury. In the room on the fourth floor which overlooked the park, Neville tipped the porter who had brought up the luggage, and asked Karen if she wanted a drink.

"Perhaps some coffee."

The coffee arrived soon afterwards. Relaxing on the sofa Karen savored the coffee's warmth as she looked out through the window to the lights of Park Lane and the dark trees beyond.

"Karen." He was beside her, his fingers touching the nape of her neck, gently taking the coffee cup from her hands and putting it on the table. "Karen."

After a while he said: "I'll put off going to Scotland. We'll go somewhere else for a week—perhaps Paris—"

"No," she said instinctively. "Not Paris."

"Where would you like to go?"

Later, long afterwards, she wondered why she did not say Madeira—Greece—Capri—anywhere where there would be no long shadows from the past, no mocking memories. Perhaps it was some obscure response to a challenge. Or perhaps it was because she knew at heart she had been running away for the past three years and now if she was to stand and face her future squarely she knew she must overcome all weakness and be so strong that nothing, not even the most violent memory from the past could hurt her any more.

April has interfered quite enough in my life, she was aware of thinking with resolution, but she won't interfere any longer. Am I to say no to a trip to Scotland every time Neville is obliged to visit Plantation Q?

"I'm not afraid of going back to Scotland," she said firmly to Neville. "And I want to exorcise April's ghost finally and forever. Let me come with you to the Plantation."

For a moment she fancied she saw a shadow in his eyes, a slight tightening of his fine mouth, and then he shrugged his shoulders with a smile and the moment of uneasiness was gone.

"As you wish," he said, and leant forward to take her in his arms.

3

Melissa returned to her apartment shortly before midnight after visiting an old schoolfriend who lived in Surrey, and found Karen's note at once. She read it once carelessly, a second time in incredulous comprehension, and a third time to make sure her eyes were not deceiving her. Then she went to the living-room, mixed herself a stiff Scotch and soda and sat down very calmly.

It was ridiculous to get upset. Ridiculous—and undignified. And humiliating. And a dozen other things which did not bear thinking about.

Melissa took a mouthful of scotch meticulously, much as a child would take abhorred medicine, and reached for a cigarette.

After all, she thought more levelly, it had only been an affair. She always took scrupulous care not to become too involved with the men in her life, and why should Neville Bennett have been different from any of the others whom she had handled with such adroit competence? The answer came flashing into her mind with a most unwelcome clarity. Because she thought, it was not she who had handled Neville; Neville had handled her. And she had been clay in his hands.

The wave of humiliation was so deep and so excruciating that she nearly crushed the glass in her hands to fragments. She had run after Neville like an adolescent; she had behaved in a manner which for a grown woman had been incredible. Her cheeks flamed as she looked back, remembering incident after incident, how

73

she had schemed to get him, schemed to keep him, schemed—even schemed to marry him. Well thank God nothing had come of that. It was incredible to think that she could ever have been so foolish over a man. Incredible, and unbearable.

The fury was edging the humiliation from her mind as she got up and began to pace up and down the room. He had taken her, used her for a year and then casually discarded her—as if she were some tramp who had served her purpose! Karen had only to crook her little finger, and . . . What did Neville see in that woman anyway? She was pretty certainly, but much too reserved and quiet. Deep, thought Melissa, seizing on the word. Yes, that was it! Deep. Still waters never ran deeper . . . All that talk about there being no possibility of a reconciliation! No doubt she had planned it all along.

Melissa finished her drink and ground her cigarette to dust in the ash tray.

It was a pity, she thought, that Karen hadn't confided in her. Melissa could have told her a thing or two about Neville Bennett.

But perhaps Karen was so infatuated that she would have refused to hear anything against Neville. Perhaps —and perhaps not. April was, after all, Karen's sister.

She considered the idea of an anonymous letter and then rejected it instantly. That would be too obvious, too lacking in subtlety, too—what was the word?—too crass. There were surely better ways of pointing out to Karen what a fool she was to go back to that man. Imagine going back to Scotland with him as well! Melissa's eyes narrowed in scorn. She felt cooler now, more composed. The anger was still with her but now it was an ice-cold controlled anger, infinitely more virulent than the first rush of rage. After a while she lit another cigarette and went to her files of correspondence which she kept in connection with the running of the boutique. She had always planned to do more research on the prices and suppliers of genuine Scottish tweeds. Tweeds always sold well, particularly to American tourists who thought such material was a typically British product. Perhaps in the autumn of next year she could bring out a comprehensive line embodying new styles of tweed, but if she decided to go ahead with such a project she would have to make a business trip to Scotland.

Pulling out her map of the British Isles she studied the section devoted to Scotland and began to calculate which was the nearest tweed mill to Plantation Q.

4

Leonie waited up for Neville till midnight and then went to bed with reluctance. She was, of course, accustomed to Neville's nights away from home and had long since learnt never to question him or even to make observations to him about them. Nonetheless she often worried in case he had had an accident in his car (most unlikely, for Neville was an excellent driver) and, in any event, she was always conscious of a faint but unmistakeable disapproval when she was reminded of this discreet but recurring aspect of Neville's private life. Her father, she thought, would not have approved at all. Their parents were long since dead, but Leonie often thought of them, particularly of her father who had been a quiet. scholarly man with no recreations outside his archaeological studies except a round of golf on Sundays and an hour's gardening from time to time. He had been ascetic, almost monastic in his way of life, very different from his witty, gay, and much too attractive wife who had been occasionally unfaithful but had never quite made the effort to leave him.

Leonie sighed in irritation, turned out the light and lay back on her pillows in the darkness.

Sleep was impossible, of course; she might have guessed as much. At two o'clock she got up, went down to the kitchen and made herself a cup of tea. In spite of herself she could not stop wondering where Neville was, which was foolish because she knew very well that he had taken Karen out to dinner and it was obvious he was set on effecting a reconciliation. No doubt by this time they were at some hotel.

Leonie closed her mind resolutely, washed up her cup and saucer and rinsed out the teapot.

Not for the first time she wondered why such antipathy existed between herself and Karen. Leonie had never liked Americans. Nasty noisy people, she thought with distaste, brash, tasteless and inexpressibly vulgar. It made no difference that Karen was quiet, charming and had excellent taste. She was one of Them. Even the accent set Leonie on edge. And she thought of Karen's brother Thomas with a shudder, Thomas with his bold, cynical, baby-blue eyes, and that appalling drawl and that indescribably awful slang—and his clothes! Thank God that at least Karen looked respectable and was fit to be presented in the circles in which Neville moved. It would have been too dreadful if Neville had married a female equivalent of Thomas. April, for instance.

Leonie allowed herself one long shudder and moved briskly upstairs. Now was not the moment to begin remembering the past. If she started thinking about that terrible weekend at the farm she would be awake all night.

Which she was. Even her sleeping pills had no effect. She tossed and turned, read a few pages of her library book, and tossed and turned again. She was thinking of Marney now, remembering times long ago and comparing them to the present, her mind full of regrets, bitterness and a useless but persistent welling of self-pity.

At five o'clock in the morning she got up and began to move about the room in an agony of restlessness. This is all Karen's fault, she thought dry-eyed; if she hadn't come back I wouldn't have started to think of the past. The past was closed and forgotten—as far as one can ever forget—and yet now she comes back to remind me, to stir up all the old memories, the pain, the shock, the horror, the humiliation.

She was crying. Tears scorched her cheeks but she made no effort to check them. I shall be pushed aside now, she was aware of thinking bitterly, just as I was when he married Karen and brought her back to his house at Cambridge. I shall have to go away and live on my own, just as I did then—and after I've found somewhere to live, what then? I shall be a middle-aged spinster, discarded, redundant, and useless. And once I leave Neville's house I know perfectly well that I shall no longer have the chance to see Marney so often;

there will be no more opportunities to speak to him on the phone.

And all because Karen had come back to London. And Neville wanted her back.

But perhaps it wouldn't last. Perhaps they would quarrel again and Karen would go back to America.

Leonie drew back the curtains to watch the dawn breaking over London. Her tears had stopped; she was calmer now, resolute and determined. She would not be usurped, she told herself tight-lipped. She would not be cast aside, discarded as valueless. She had her own life to lead, didn't she? She would show Karen that it would not be easy to push her out of the way: Karen would be surprised when she found out how awkward Leonie could make the situation.

Dawn had broken; the sun was rising. Suddenly exhausted, Leonie lay down again on the bed, and this time, all her anger spent, she slept until the child bounced into her room at seven o'clock to ask her where his father was.

5

Marney did not usually go to the office on Saturdays, but this time was an exception. His superior, a very senior gentleman in the current government, was expecting a report from him on an industrial concern in the north which was experimenting with a certain type of lumber; there was a debate in the House next week and the Minister must, absolutely must, have the report by Monday morning. Marney had sighed in resignation, wondered for the twentieth time why he had left the peace of academic life, and buckled down to his duties as a civil servant. He had just finished the last page of the report and was relaxing in relief when there was a knock on his door and Neville walked in.

Marney raised his eyebrows. Here was a different Neville, vibrant yet relaxed, as sleek and content as a well-fed tomcat. Marney felt his mouth twist ironically in the second before the shock made his heart miss a beat.

"So there you are!" said Neville lightly. "I thought I remembered you saying you would be working this morning. I just dropped in to collect my file on Plantation Q. We're off to Scotland on Monday."

"We?"

"Karen and I."

The paper clip between Marney's fingers bent into a contorted fantasy and broke. Marney smiled. "Congratulations," he said pleasantly.

Neville grinned like a schoolboy, tossed back the lock of dark hair which had fallen over his forehead and flung himself down in the chair by the desk. "Surprised?"

"A little. But not unduly."

"I thought I'd phone Symons and tell him I'm taking five days' leave. That means I can have a complete week with Karen alone at the farm before I have to bother to go over to the lodge on Plantation Q and do business with Kelleher. The business isn't urgent, after all. I've been putting it off for the last month so it won't hurt to put it off a week longer."

"True. In that case, why not go somewhere else for a week?"

"Karen decided against that."

"Oh?"

"Well, first of all I thought I would make a business trip of it from start to finish, and then when Karen said she didn't mind coming I thought I would postpone the business for a few days."

"I see."

"I've just been talking to Leonie about it, actually. We both wanted Snuff to come with us, but then decided it might be better if he joined us when I began my business at the Plantation. Karen and I'll have a few days together first. Fortunately Leonie's volunteered to bring Snuff up to the farm herself so we don't have to worry about how he's going to get there."

"That was good of her."

"Well, it wasn't exactly what I had in mind, but it's certainly the best way of getting Snuff up to the farm since he's too young to travel so far on his own. Besides, I couldn't tell Leonie not to come because in fact, if you remember, the farm does belong to her. When I bought it I gave it to her by deed of gift as a tax dodge, and of course in the end she did go there often before Karen and I were married—she used to spend about two months of the year there, and even now she goes up for visits during the summer."

"I would have thought it an asset to have her at the farm when you begin work at the Plantation," Marney said without emphasis. "It'll be lonely for Karen on her own there during the day."

"Well, yes, there is that to it, I suppose, but they've never got on too well, unfortunately . . . What really worries me is what I'm to say to Leonie when we come back from Plantation Q. I think it would be fatal if she continued to live with us, especially since she can't or won't get on with Karen, but so far she hasn't volunteered to look for a flat of her own. I can foresee an awkward situation developing."

"Tedious for you," said Marney.

"Very. Still . . ." He rose to his feet lithely and wandered back to the door. "There's no sense in worrying about it now, I suppose. I'll see you in about a fortnight's time, Marney. Phone me if an emergency crops up on any of my projects, but I'm not expecting any trouble at the moment."

"All right. Give my regards to Karen, won't you? Tell her I'm delighted everything's ended happily."

"Ended?" laughed Neville. "It's just beginning!"

"I suppose so. Goodbye, Neville."

" 'Bye." The door slammed. Footsteps sauntered off down the passage.

Marney took a deep breath.

He stood up, conscientiously reminding himself that Neville was his oldest friend, but he still felt indignant. Beyond the window lay the lush green of the lawns and trees of St. James's Park, the glint of water glimpsed through the trees, the strolling Londoners relaxing on their day off. Marney turned back to his desk, collected the sheaf of papers which constituted his report and clipped the pages together. His hand, he noticed to his astonishment, was shaking. How extraordinary! He had known for twenty-five years that Neville was the type of man who always got what he wanted, so why should Marney now of all times feel so indignant because Neville had achieved the desired reconciliation with his wife and was frank enough to admit he now found his sister redundant? Neville was only conforming to his usual pattern of behavior. Why should Marney feel so angry?

It was because of Karen, of course. Marney admired Karen and was fond of her. He had admired her even more when she had done what no woman had ever done before, when she had walked out on Neville Bennett and refused to go back to him. The fact that she had consented so willingly now to a reconciliation was somehow an immense disappointment; Marney felt disillusioned. Perhaps Karen was the same as any other woman after all and he had overestimated her when he had considered her unique in relation to Neville.

He put on his raincoat, opened the door abruptly and stepped out into the corridor. He still felt angry, he realized, and what was worse he was aware of a contempt mingled with disgust which was somehow directed against his friend. Moving downstairs quickly he went outside and crossed the road into the park, but the feeling persisted, shamefully identifiable and profoundly uncomfortable.

He reached the bridge over the long lake and paused half-way across to look east at the fairytale skyline which was one of the most celebrated views of any city. The sun was shining; the sky was blue. And before him above the lake and the fringes of trees rose the towers and minarets of Horseguards, eastern, mysterious, cosmopolitan.

Be honest, he told himself, admit it. You're jealous of Neville, you always were and you always will be. Admit it and live with it and laugh it off but don't, for God's sake, let it fester and seeth and corrupt.

It was three years since he had had to reason with

himself like this. Three long years. He had thought he had purged himself of all jealousy, cauterized himself of all hatred and resentment. He had thought that never again would he even feel the desire to let his emotions govern his civilized self-control or lose his grip on his sense of proportion, yet now here he was again, dizzy with the corrosive emotion he despised, willing himself to be sensible and realistic while the old scars he thought healed broke open and scorched his memory with their poison.

But he must not think of April. She was part of the past. It was foolish now to think of her and remember the part she had played in his life.

He turned blindly and walked off the bridge. None of this would have happened, he thought, if Karen had remained in America. Three years of peace, of learning to forget, and now this.

At least, he thought in relief as he reached the Mall and began to walk towards Trafalgar Square, at least this time he wouldn't be at Plantation Q.

6

Six days passed.

It was the following Friday at four in the afternoon when Thomas Conway reached Paris, installed himself in a modest but comfortable hotel, and placed a phone call to Melissa's apartment where he thought his sister was staying. Melissa, home early from her boutique, answered the phone.

"Hi Melissa—how are you?" In common with numerous Americans he never bothered to announce who he was at the beginning of a telephone conversation. The curious part was that most of the people he telephoned seemed to have no trouble in identifying him unaided.

"Thomas, I presume," enquired Melissa, running true to form.

"In person. I'm calling from Paris and hope to fix a free plane ride to London tomorrow . . . Is Karen there?"

"No," said Melissa, very cool. "She left a week ago."

"What!" shouted Thomas. "You mean she went home so soon? Why the hell did she do that?"

"No, she hasn't gone home actually." Melissa sounded crisply composed. "She's gone to Scotland, to Plantation Q."

There was a silence. Then: "You have to be kidding," said Thomas at last. "You have to be."

"No, I'm perfectly serious. They went there a week ago."

"You mean she and Neville—"

"Yes, they had a reconciliation."

"My God," said Thomas.

"They were reconciled last Friday—exactly a week ago, in fact. Then on Saturday Karen called to tell me she and Neville would be in Scotland for a fortnight or so—Neville had business at the Plantation but they planned a few days alone together at the farm first. Leonie's flying up to Inverness tomorrow with the child to join them."

"But Scotland!" said Thomas appalled. "That goddamned Plantation!"

"I suppose she wanted to prove to herself that she could go back there again."

"She's nuts."

Melissa sounded slightly amused. "Perhaps."

"Look, can I stop by at your place when I get to London tomorrow?"

"That depends when you're arriving. I'm setting off for Scotland myself tomorrow, and I plan to leave at nine-thirty."

"Yeah?" He was interested. "Vacation?"

"Business. I want to visit a tweed mill near Fort William."

"Fort William? Isn't that near—hey, want a co-driver?"

He really was a confirmed sponger, Melissa observed dispassionately. Unless she was careful she would be paying his overnight hotel bill as well as providing him with a free ride to see his sister.

"Well, I must say," she said, affecting relief mingled with pleasure. "I would appreciate someone to help with the driving—have you ever driven a Fiat 600 before—and of course I'd appreciate your help with the petrol expenses too. That would be wonderful, Thomas."

If he was disappointed at her hint, he gave no sign of it. "I'll get a night flight tonight," he said. "I'll call the airport right now. Maybe I could come direct to your apartment when I arrive? If Karen's not there maybe I could use your spare room to save all the trouble of finding a hotel. You wouldn't mind, would you?"

Melissa did mind, very much. "Well—"

"That's all right," said Thomas comfortably. "I won't ask for anything I shouldn't."

Melissa, who had fended off a couple of routine attempts at seduction by Thomas when they had first met several years ago in New York, was not so sure.

"You think it over," he said winningly. "You've got my guarantee of good behavior. With luck I'll see you before midnight. 'Bye now."

The line clicked as he replaced the receiver. Melissa stared at the telephone in distaste and then shrugged her shoulders philosophically. Perhaps after all the situation could be turned to her advantage.

7

At about the same time in the office on Birdcage Walk, Marney was closing a file and looking forward to a pleasantly peaceful weekend. He was still looking forward to the weekend when the door opened and his superior walked into the room.

"Dr. West, something's come up in relation to Plantation Q . . .

" . . . just received a call from Kelleher at the foresters' lodge . . ."

His muscles slowly tightened.

" . . . Neville Bennett's up there right now, of course, but he doesn't have any of the files on the syndrome, nor is he particularly well-acquainted with them since they are, after all, your project—"

Horror made the room blur before his eyes. A very polite voice which he dimly recognized as his own was saying: "Sir, is it really necessary for me to go? I'm very tied up at the moment with the White Paper. Perhaps Wilkins—"

"Wilkins is in Scandinavia. No, it'll have to be you, I'm afraid. But it won't be for long. Let's see, if you flew up tomorrow you could be at the lodge in the evening—I'll send a wire to Kelleher to have one of the men meet you at Inverness airport. A couple of days should put matters right."

Marney listened, acquiesced, noted down his instructions with meticulous precision. Then when he was alone at last he sat for a long while at his desk before standing up, putting on his raincoat and stowing into his briefcase the files necessary for his unexpected, unwanted visit to Plantation Q.

Four

1

The lake was in the remote regions of the Western Highlands near the sea-loch of Hourn and bordering the vast territories of Lochiel. It was a little lake, small and peaceful, and the road wound all along one side of it from Kildoun to the junction of the road to Kyle of Lochalsh many miles away. The converted farm which Neville had bought and given to his sister some years ago lay on the opposite side of the lake to the road; decades earlier the lake had been fordable, but the modern age with its hydro-electric schemes had put an end to that and now a boat was necessary to cross the lake from the farm to the road; Neville kept two rowing boats for convenience's sake, and the farm had a small jetty and boathouse. Leonie had tended the small patch of ground nearby with great patience, and now a few hardy flowers flourished spasmodically in the beds beneath the windows. However, her pride and joy was the rockery which she had built some yards from the house, and it was here that her gardening talents had been most successful.

From behind the farm, a rough track climbed sharply up the mountainside and eventually surmounted the ridge to lead down into the next valley to the foresters' lodge at Plantation Q. The Q stood for Question-mark, for it was an experimental plantation, and Neville was often obliged to visit it to see how the trees were growing and to supervise the implementing of new schemes. From the lodge at the Plantation, an estate road ran a winding four-mile course to join the main road to Fort William and a hint of civilization.

Neville and Karen had arrived at Inverness airport without incident the previous Monday and had been met in person by Kelleher, who was in charge at the foresters' lodge. A trained forester with years of experience in Canada and Norway, he drove an ancient, but aristocratic, Rolls Royce on all expeditions away from the Plantation, and it was in this grizzled old motor car that Neville and Karen were taken to Plantation Q. Here they had dinner with Kelleher and the foresters and botanists who staffed the lodge, and then Neville borrowed one of the fleet of jeeps to drive over the mountains to the little lake and the converted farm.

"Everything's ready for you," Kelleher told them. "As soon as your wire came on Saturday, I contacted Mrs. MacLeod and she and her daughter went over and aired the house and saw that everything was in order. I drove over yesterday with a supply of food and

the place looked all right to me. If you need anything
more just give us a ring and I'll send one of the boys
over in a jeep."

But everything was perfect. They had set off in the
jeep from the lodge and Karen, who had privately
dreaded the arrival at the farm, found that the drive
was so breathtaking that even her fears were eclipsed.
They reached the boundary of the plantation, surmounted the pass, and then Neville stopped the jeep
for a moment to look at the view. There was a full
moon. White light steamed across the bare moorland of
the valley before them: far below was the long slender
gleam of the lake. Everywhere was quite still, absolutely at peace, and Karen caught her breath and felt the
unexpected tears prick her eyes because it was so
beautiful.

"I'm glad we came back," she said.

He found her hand and held it tightly for a second
before they drove on.

The farm at first appeared to be set by the water's
edge and it was only when they drew nearer that it became apparent that it was set more than a hundred
yards back from the lake on rising ground. The walls
were whitewashed, and in the darkness it was impossible to tell which were the original walls of the one-
room cottage and which were the walls which had been
added when the building had been enlarged. Nearby,
the cascading white waters of the creek roared downhill
to meet the lake. After Neville had parked the jeep,
Karen followed him across the wooden bridge, passed
Leonie's rockery and so came at last to the back door
of the cottage.

Neville lit a lamp and then went back for the remaining suitcases, but Karen took the lamp and walked through the kitchen, through the small dining-room into the living-room. Everywhere looked just the same. She tried for a moment to picture April there, but to her surprise could not. Neville was right, she thought to herself. There were no ghosts.

And she was conscious of a great relief as all the tensions ebbed at last from her mind.

She went upstairs to the main bedroom, took off her coat and removed the counterpane from the bed. The sheets looked crisp and inviting. Slipping off her shoes she lay down and closed her eyes and so complete was her relaxation that she drifted into sleep almost at once and did not even hear Neville bring the suitcases upstairs. The next thing she knew was that he was beside her, his lips seeking hers, his arms pressing her closer to him, and it seemed to her for one bizarre moment that the past three years had been a dream and that she had just awoken after a long sleep; perhaps April had never come to the farm, perhaps none of the terrible scenes of three years ago had ever happened . . .

"Happy?" she heard Neville murmur at last.

"Mmmm . . ." And she was. Tonight for the first time the reconciliation seemed a reality.

Later he said: "Tonight at last you seemed to love me without reservations."

The match flared as he lit a cigarette; she saw his face for a moment in the darkness, but as the match died there was only the moonlight streaming through the uncurtained window, the tranquility, the peace.

"It wasn't easy at the hotel."

"I know."

"I felt more like your mistress than your wife."

"I should have waited till we got here—"

"I was impatient too, don't forget!"

They laughed. He leant over and kissed her. After a long while he said: "This marks the new beginning, then. A new life together, new happiness, new everything. Children too, if you wish. And the past is never, never going to come between us again."

But the past was there all the same. In the daylight the memories seemed sharper. She went down to the jetty the next morning and the boats reminded her of how Thomas had rowed her across the lake three years ago; she walked a short way up the track past the rockery behind the house and found herself remembering the morning when she had escaped from Neville and April at the farm and rushed blindly up the track towards Plantation Q. And most horrible of all, she went into the tumbled-down, deserted cottage further down the lakeside, and the atmosphere of crumbling decay reminded her unreasonably of Melissa's wild insinuations, the suggestion that April was still somewhere near the farm despite everyone's assumption that she had gone away. Karen shivered violently. She glanced around her again, but there was nothing there, only the moist walls of the cottage, the soft earthen floor littered with weeds and rubble, the sightless windows which faced the calm waters of the lake. But the next moment she was running, the breath tearing at her lungs, and when she met Neville at the door of the cottage she clung to him in relief even as she laughed at her ridiculous state of panic.

The days passed uneventfully. The weather was moderately good; it rained a little every day, but there was some sunshine too, usually in the afternoons, and the evening sunsets were magnificent, a blaze of scarlet and pink behind the mountain peaks. Neville took her boating and fishing, to the hotel at Kildoun for a drink and dinner, to Fort William to shop for provisions. They went for long walks up the stream or by the lake, explored the vast tracts of moors, discovered old paths in the heather. When it was wet they relaxed by the peat fire in the living-room, played records on the ancient gramophone which had to be wound by hand, or listened to the transistor radio.

But the past was still there. Despite herself, Karen was conscious of it, and although she sought to rationalize her awareness of memory she wasn't altogether successful. After all, it was impossible that she should remember nothing of what had happened three years ago, she told herself sensibly. One couldn't expect a convenient amnesia. Some memory was inevitable, but what was important was that it shouldn't matter, shouldn't upset her in any way.

Yet the sense of discomfort persisted and grew.

It was more a sense of anticipation than anything else, an intuitive core of dread lodged at the back of her mind. As the week drew to a close she diverted herself by thinking that Leonie would be there presently with Snuff and the arrival would shift the past further out of sight, but even as she thought this another part of her mind was saying: Leonie was here three years ago. To some extent her presence will recreate the horror of that other weekend.

Then came the news of Marney's pending arrival, and her dread deepened.

"He'll be staying at the lodge, of course," said Neville carelessly, as if he guessed the cause of her anxiety, but his words held no comfort for her.

Marney had stayed at the lodge last time.

She tried to pull herself together, told herself that it was absurd to see any relationship between the coming weekend and the weekend that had ended her marriage three years ago. Neville made arrangements by phone for Leonie to hire a car which would meet her at the airport when she arrived with Snuff, and Karen busied herself determinedly about the house, dusting, cleaning and cooking in readiness for the visitors. By the time they arrived she was well in command of herself, and seeing the child again took her mind away from her worries.

Marney reached Plantation Q that evening and telephoned Neville from the lodge, but this made little impression on her.

And then without any warning, Melissa and Thomas arrived on Sunday night at Kildoun.

2

Marney had driven over for dinner that evening, and it was he who answered the phone when the call came through. Leonie was in the kitchen making coffee and Karen had just taken Snuff up to bed. Neville was sitting in the armchair by the fire, his legs stretched out before the hearth, his hands clasped behind his head as he yawned, while Marney was changing the needle on the antique gramophone.

The bell rang.

"I'll get it," said Marney. "It's probably Kelleher." He picked up the extension receiver. "Hello? Dr. West speaking."

"Hi Marney," said Thomas amiably. "How are you? Karen around?"

"Thomas? Well, this is a surprise! Just a moment, please." He put down the receiver.

"Who?" exclaimed Neville incredulously.

"A male American accent asking for Karen."

"Good God!" He was on his feet, moving over to the phone while Marney went out of the room to fetch Karen. "Thomas? Neville. Where are you phoning from?"

"Just across the lake." Neville heard him turn aside to speak to someone else. "What's the name of this place, honey? I never could remember . . . Kildoun. I had a lucky break and got a lift all the way from London. Do you remember a friend of Karen's called Melissa Fleming?"

Karen was right behind him. "What's the matter, Neville?"

Neville said disbelievingly: "Thomas is at Kildoun with Melissa."

Karen stared at him. There was a silence. Presently the receiver began to shout at them in a little faraway voice: "Neville? Hey, what's happened! Neville, are you there? Neville—"

Karen took the receiver. "Calm down, Thomas, and stop having hysterics. How are you, and how did you get here? What a wonderful surprise!"

Thomas, slightly mollified, settled down to explain. He had gone to London, found Melissa was about to depart on a business trip to a mill near Fort William and had managed to persuade her to drive a few miles further north so that he could be delivered almost to the door.

"Wasn't that nice of her? Hey, Karen, why don't we come on over? Is there a boat this side we could use?"

"Let me check with Neville." She muffled the receiver against her breast. "They want to come over."

"Both of them?"

"Apparently."

"Good God—"

"I suppose Melissa hasn't told him anything at all. Neville, I can't refuse him—I haven't seen him for three years—"

"Of course. Let me talk to him." He took the receiver. "Thomas, I'll row over myself and pick you up— expect me in about fifteen minutes' time. Incidentally, I'm afraid we can't invite you and Melissa to stay as Leonie and Snuff are here and there's no room—would it be all right if you stayed at the hotel in Kildoun?"

"I guess that shouldn't be any problem."

"Good. In that case I don't suppose Melissa wants to be bothered with coming over, does she? Perhaps some time tomorrow—"

"You want to come, Melissa? They've no room for us to stay . . . You do? Okay. Neville? Yes, Melissa says she'll come over for the ride. See you in fifteen minutes then. Thanks a lot."

The line went dead.

"God damn that woman," said Neville, slamming the receiver back into its cradle, his face scarlet with rage.

"God damn her."

"Is she coming?"

"Of course she's coming! Do you think she'd miss

the opportunity to play the role of Woman Scorned? She's enjoying every minute of her petty little vendetta!"

"Well, don't give her the pleasure of seeing she's upset you," said Karen levelly. "Pretend you're amused, if anything. Make out that you don't give a damn." Neville's fury had the effect of making her calmer than she would otherwise have been, but when he left the room a moment later to get a sweater and change his shoes, she felt the panic edge down her spine. Thomas, Marney, Neville and Leonie were back once more with her in Scotland; only Melissa had had no part in that weekend of three years ago.

The child called from upstairs and she pulled herself together and went back to him. It was foolish to become neurotic over what was merely an unfortunate coincidence.

Neville set off, still looking angry, and presently when Karen had returned downstairs to the living-room Leonie brought in the coffee. Half an hour passed. Marney was just putting more fuel on the fire when they heard the sound of voices outside and the next moment the front door was opening and Neville was leading the way into the living-room.

"Karen!" shouted Thomas in delight, and embraced his sister with a fervor which made the English spectators stare in surprise. He stepped back a pace admiringly. "You look great!"

He himself looked better than would most travelers who had spent a week gravitating from one side of Europe to the other. He was immaculately dressed; clothes looked well on Thomas and he wasn't ashamed of looking smart and fashionable. He spent a great deal of money on his wardrobe, but considered it money well invested since in his profession it was important to keep up appearances. He wasn't tall, but he was tall enough to be able to describe himself as five foot eleven and be believed. He had a vague air of being in excellent physical condition; his dark hair was short but not crew-cut and curled in exactly the right places, his mouth was slightly crooked, and his nose, broken in adolescence, had healed attractively. He had a scar on his left cheek of which he was proud, but apart from this idiosyncrasy he was not unduly vain.

"I smell coffee," he said, sniffing like a dog. "Just what I need! Have you eaten yet, by the way? I'm starved."

"Thomas," said Melissa, almost but not quite embarrassed, "you're entirely shameless."

"I'll go and get you something, Thomas," said Karen. "Melissa, would you—"

"Just coffee, darling. We had sandwiches at the hotel just now but Thomas seems to have forgotten about them."

"I'm going to have a drink," said Neville. "What about you, Marney? Will you have a whisky with me?"

Karen escaped to the kitchen and heard footsteps padding along behind her.

"Where's the light-switch?" muttered Thomas, feeling the wall in the darkness. Then, as memory returned: "My God, you mean to say they've got no electricity here? Isn't that hydro-electric scheme finished yet?"

"Neville didn't bother to have electricity put in. He figured it wasn't worth it as he didn't live here permanently." She lit a lamp and turned up the wick so that the kitchen was illuminated with a gloomy brightness. "How about some cold ham or chicken with salad?"

"Delicious." He watched, sharp-eyed as a lynx, as she began to move about the kitchen. "Well, well," he said at last. "Who would ever have thought that we'd meet again here? Who would have thought three years ago that here we'd all be again three years later—"

"I suppose you're surprised I agreed to come back."

"Surprised?" said Thomas. "Yes, I was surprised. I'll tell you something else. I was more than surprised. I was stupefied and amazed and began to have serious doubts about your sanity."

"Thomas!" She had to laugh. "Just because I didn't take your advice—"

"Hell, I wasn't so naive as to think you would, but I thought there was no harm in trying. I guessed that if you once saw him again you'd be right back where you started. You're a sensible girl, Karen—you don't have to convince me of that—and your judgment of men was always so damned impeccable that it was irritating, but even sensible girls have their blind spots, and Neville Bennett just happens to be yours. Okay, fair enough! It's your life and if he makes you happy, that's swell, but he didn't make you very happy the other time, did he, and I don't know why you should think he'll make you any happier now than the time before."

"Oh, stop that, Thomas—"

"Honey, I've met men like Neville before—you find them often enough in the acting profession, strange as that may seem to you. They're handsome and smart and charming and they're all hell with the women, but you know something? You know who they really love better than anyone else in all the big wide world? No, *not* their mothers—not their wives—not even their mistresses. They're in love with themselves. They love their cute little selves better than anything else on this earth, and—"

"Surely not as much as you love the sound of your own voice, Thomas," said Neville blandly from the doorway.

Thomas swung round.

Oh God, thought Karen. The carving knife slipped from her fingers and fell to the floor with a clatter.

"You'd better let me do that," said Neville, moving forward. He picked up the carving knife, wiped it clean and turned to the chicken on the draining board.

Thomas said idly: "How's the kid? May I see him?"

"Why, yes, of course!" Karen grasped at the diversion with such relief that she was afraid afterwards she might have sounded too pleased. "I'm surprised he hasn't ventured downstairs to inspect the new arrivals. Come up and say hello to him."

They escaped upstairs.

"You *are* a fool, Thomas!" whispered Karen wretchedly. "What on earth did you want to say all that for? And besides, it's not true any more—you had no right—"

"Okay, okay, I'm sorry." Thomas had the grace to look contrite. "But how was I to know he'd come sneaking into the kitchen after us? Look, after we've seen the kid let's go outside for a stroll where no one will disturb us. I want to talk to you."

Snuff, evidently overcome with the excitement of being in a new place and the strength of the Highland air, was fast asleep.

"That explains why he didn't come down to see

you," she murmured to Thomas. "I think we'd better wait till tomorrow."

They returned cautiously to the kitchen. A lamp was still burning and there was a plate of newly-carved chicken on the draining-board, but Neville had evidently returned to the living-room. Thomas picked up a slice of chicken absent-mindedly and moved to the back door.

"Let's go across the creek a little way."

"Burn," said Karen automatically, reaching for the coat which hung on the back of the door. "You're not in Minnesota now."

They went outside. Across the creek they took the track up the mountainside and after about five minutes found a flat rock where they could sit and survey the sweep of the moors and the lighted windows of the farmhouse below.

"I hope you haven't got mixed up with Melissa, Thomas," said Karen presently.

He was scandalized. "Melissa? Now, wait awhile—"

"Since you so kindly advised me about my private life I thought I'd return the compliment and advise you about yours," said Karen dryly. "And since you must have spent about forty-eight hours in Melissa's company, and bearing in mind that you must have stopped over somewhere last night—"

"Separate rooms," said Thomas.

"And the night before?"

"I had your room at her apartment. Hey, what *is* this?"

"And nothing happened?"

"And nothing happened," said Thomas virtuously.

"But I bet you tried!" She was teasing him now, a

smile hovering at the corners of her mouth. "What a blow to your ego!"

"Well, of course I tried," said Thomas crossly. "Why not? But I might have guessed it was a waste of time. She was always cold, even when I first met her."

"She was warm enough to please Neville for over a year."

His mouth dropped open. He looked so comical in his surprise that she laughed out loud.

"You're kidding."

"No, it's true. He was just trying to end the affair discreetly when I arrived."

"Well, I'm damned . . ." He brooded on the information for a moment. Then: "But in that case what the hell's she doing here?"

"I was hoping you were going to tell me. I suppose she's just malicious and seized on the opportunity to make Neville feel embarrassed."

"Neville!" said Thomas. "Neville! Who cares about Neville? You're the one she's embarrassing!"

"If she really is acting out of malice, I just feel sorry for her making such a futile exhibition of herself."

"That's amazing," reflected Thomas. "To think that I've been traveling with her for two days and she never once mentioned her relationship with Neville. You'd have thought she'd have said something bitchy which would have given her away."

"Melissa's much too clever for that."

"But we talked a lot about Neville," said Thomas. "We both agreed——" He stopped.

"Well, go on," said Karen. "Don't stop. I know what you think about Neville, and I can guess what she must be feeling by this time. What did you agree?"

"Only that we thought you were—ill-advised to return to him," said Thomas with reluctance. "We talked of April—she asked me exactly what had happened . . ."

"Did she suggest that April was dead?"

He looked at her quickly in the darkness. "Did she suggest that to you?"

"She mentioned it was a possibility."

"Well, it is possible, I guess."

"Here in Scotland?"

"It would explain one or two puzzling things." He was hedging, defensive.

"Did she think it was an accident?"

"We—mentioned something about that—"

"You mean," said Karen, "that between you, you agreed that April's dead and Neville murdered her."

"For Christ's sake, Karen—"

"That's too much, Thomas!" She felt all the more angry because she recognized the panic trembling at the back of her mind. "It's slander and you know it, and how you dare, how you have the nerve to suggest such a thing when we have no proof that April's even dead—"

"But listen, Karen," interrupted Thomas. "Before you get really excited, just think for a moment. Go back step by step over what happened three years ago, and you'll see that there are one or two strange angles to the situation. Forget the possibility that she was murdered. Just concentrate on the possibility that she's dead."

"I don't want to," Karen said stubbornly, and in spite of herself she shivered. "I won't."

"Look," said Thomas patiently. "Nobody's saying Neville killed her. Say I killed her, if it'll make you feel any happier. Lord knows I felt like it often enough from the age of two onwards—you know we never got along together. I think in some ways—but not all, thank God—we were more alike than any of the rest of the family; we were certainly the two black sheep of the all-white batch, and because we were alike I always saw right through her. She might have fooled you, Karen, but she didn't fool me. She wasn't just a bitch and a phoney—she was a parasite exploiting you whenever she felt you had something to offer—"

"No," said Karen instinctively. "It wasn't like that."

"Unfortunately it was," said Thomas with unexpected firmness, "and half your troubles sprang from the fact that you refused to admit it. You can play the part of the ostrich much too well if you want to, Karen, but please don't play it now. Take a good long cool look at the possibility of April's death. To start with, if she's alive where is she? I've sounded the grapevine, even called up one or two of the producers she used to run around with. Nothing. They'd almost forgotten who she was. I haven't heard from her, you haven't heard from her, the family hasn't heard from her. So if she's alive what the hell's she doing? Okay, so she might have found herself some rich man and be living quietly in retirement—I concede that that's possible, but even if that's true I still think it's odd that she hasn't contacted any of her old friends to parade in front of them in mink and demonstrate her good fortune. You know how April loved to show off. Conversely if she was ill or starving you can be sure we'd have heard from her. She'd know Mother and Dad would always pay her medical bills and take her back with everything forgiven and forgotten.

"Secondly, if she's alive that means she must have left the farm that same morning that you found her with Neville. She was there when I rowed you across the lake at nine-thirty and yet Melissa tells me that by the time Leonie returned to the farm an hour and a half later after a visit to the lodge to see Marney, the farm was deserted. You were lost somewhere on Plantation Q, Neville was looking for you and I had gone back to the hotel at Kildoun to wait for your phone call to tell me what had happened. (Incidentally, I still think I should have insisted on landing with you and walking up to the cottage! I know it was none of my business, but my God, I'd have told the two of them where to go!) Anyway, during that hour and a half April must have left the farm—if she ever left—and got away. Now what puzzles me is why ever did she choose that time to leave? She'd succeeded in her plans to drive a wedge between you and Neville and she would shortly have Neville to herself for as long as she wanted. Why walk out just when she was on the brink of victory? It doesn't make sense."

"Neville had quarreled with her. He was full of remorse and told her to go."

"So he says."

"Look, Thomas—"

"Okay, we'll take the situation from another angle. April decides to leave—never mind why. Now as we both know, the farm is not just one of those places where you can walk outside on to a main highway, stand at a bus stop and get public transport in a couple of minutes. It's a very hard place to leave on the spur of the moment. You either have to walk over to Plantation Q by the trail over the mountain—an uphill hike

which April couldn't possibly have attempted with high
heels and a couple of suitcases—and then get a lift
from someone at the lodge to the railroad station at
Fort William, or else you have to row across the lake
and hang around outside Kildoun until some driver in a
passing car takes pity on you. Now can you honestly
imagine April teetering down to the jetty with her suitcases, stepping into the boat without falling in, and rowing—actually rowing—across the lake? It took Neville a quarter of an hour to row across this evening,
and Neville's a man in good physical condition. April
hated rowing always and couldn't even row for five
minutes, let alone for fifteen or twenty-five."

"If she were desperate—"

"Why on earth should she be desperate? As I've already said, why should she even go away? If I were her
and had wanted to leave in a hurry I would have done
one of two things. Either I would have phoned the
lodge and asked if there was a spare jeep and an off-
duty forester who could come over the mountain, take
me to Plantation Q and then give me another lift on to
Fort William, or I would have called the hotel at Kildoun and asked if they could send over someone to
pick me up in his boat and row me across the lake.
People don't mind hiring out their boats now and then
to make a bit of extra money—the boat I hired to row
you across the lake that day belonged to a farmer. But
April didn't do either of those two things. If she'd
called the lodge we would have heard about it, and she
didn't make use of a hired boat."

"Exactly! One of Neville's two row-boats was on
the Kildoun side of the lake so that proves she must

have rowed herself across no matter now unlikely that seems to us now."

"That doesn't prove anything," said Thomas at once. "That boat could have been towed across by himself in the second boat who then rowed himself back to the croft again. In other words the boat situation could have been rigged to make everyone think that April had gone away."

"Someone at Kildoun might have seen the boat towed across."

"So what? As far as they know the boat might have been towed across there for some visitor expected at the farm. Anyway, probably no one saw anything—Kildoun is such a tiny place and always seems so deserted. What a pity my hotel room didn't face the lake! If it had I would probably have seen exactly what happened, but all I did was sit by the bedside and wait for your call to come through. I didn't even dare leave the room for fear you'd try to get through to me when I wasn't there."

"And then finally I called you from the foresters' lodge and asked you to drive round to Plantation Q to collect me and take me away." The memory still hurt even now. Her heart ached for a moment before she pulled herself together. "But that was much later," she said abruptly. "It must have been nearly one o'clock when I called you."

"And meanwhile April had disappeared." He stared moodily out into the dusk. "I'm sorry, Karen, but I still think she's dead. I know you don't want to think that, but—"

"You mean someone killed her."

"Well—"

"Neville, for instance."

Thomas looked at her warily. "Or Leonie. She never liked April. Incidentally, why was Leonie at the farm then? I can't see why Neville arranged a rendezvous with April if he knew his sister was going to be there."

"There was no rendezvous. Leonie was on vacation there when Neville came up on business. As for April, Neville says she chased up there after him, and I—well, I believe him. April had already figured my marriage wasn't going so well and fancied the idea of stepping into my shoes. She wouldn't have waited for an invitation to spend a few days alone with Neville— she was quite capable of following him and issuing the invitation herself. She didn't realize till too late that Leonie was at the farm and Neville wasn't alone there after all."

"True." Thomas couldn't help chuckling to himself as he pictured the scene. "Imagine Leonie's face when April arrived!"

"Yes, I'll bet she was upset. I think that might have been why she set out for the lodge to see Marney the very next morning after they arrived. I expect she wanted to have a good grumble and it would have given her a convenient excuse to see him."

Thomas said idly: "Do you know if she really did see him that morning?"

"I've no idea. I should imagine so. Why?"

"Just wondering."

Karen stared out across the valley. The moon had risen and turned the dark waters of the lake to silver.

Clouds floated past the shadowy mountain peaks to the north and wreathed the black moorland in eerie shades of light and darkness.

"Melissa's wondering too," she said with irony, and added with a flash of bitterness: "I'd like to know just what kind of game she's playing right now, first planting insinuations in my mind and then following me here."

"Could it be that she wants to scare you off Neville so that she could have him back? Perhaps she thought that if she could make it seem as though he killed your sister you would be horrified enough to retreat to America again."

"Even if I did, and I certainly don't intend to, he wouldn't go back to her."

"Yes, he would," said Thomas cynically. "If he found himself alone again and there she was ready, willing and able, the least he would do would be to give the situation a new try. I would. Any man would. It's common sense."

Karen opened her mouth to object to this, but then closed it again; she didn't feel inclined to argue with him on such an intricate subject. "Shall we go?" she asked after a pause. "It's getting chilly up here, and we've been talking a long time."

He agreed in silence and helped her to her feet. Presently he said: "You think it's going to work this time with Neville?"

"I know it is."

He was uncomfortable suddenly. She was so convinced, so certain.

"He's changed, Thomas. He seems less selfish, less concerned for himself. If it were possible I'd say he wanted the reconciliation even more than I did."

"I see."

"And I can tell you this, Thomas. If April was killed, and no matter what you or Melissa say I don't believe she was, then Neville wasn't the one who killed her. That I do know."

"Which Neville are you speaking of?" he couldn't help saying. "The new Neville, who's determined to make your marriage succeed, or the old one who was so determined to drive it on to the rocks?"

"He had no reason to kill April."

"Ever heard of a 'crime passionel'? Ever heard of blackmail? Ever heard of—"

"He didn't kill her, Thomas. I know it. Neville's not a murderer."

"We're all potential murderers," he said wryly. "Some just have more opportunity for realizing the potential than others, that's all."

She didn't answer and he knew he had upset her.

"I'm sorry," he said at once. "I don't mean to say all these things against Neville. If he can make you happy, then I'm willing to be the best brother-in-law a man ever had. If I say anything against Neville it's only because I'm worried silly about you—I want you to be happy more than anything else in the world, Karen, and I'd go to great lengths to see that you were happy. You know that."

"I know," she said. "I know, Thomas."

She took his hand and they went down the steep hillside together, not speaking but conscious that they understood each other. At the back door once more,

Karén turned to him with a smile in which he glimpsed a flicker of relief.

"I'm so very glad you're here, Thomas," she said simply at last, and something in her expression made him wonder just how far she really did believe her husband to be uninvolved in April's disappearance.

Five

1

The cottage was very quiet. In the living-room Neville
was sitting alone by the fire, a novel in his hands, the
radio murmuring a Beethoven quartet. He looked up as
they came in.

"You were gone a hell of a long time," he said pleasantly, more to Thomas than to Karen. "Melissa decided not to wait for you and Marney volunteered to row
her across the lake. Leonie's gone to bed, but I thought
I might as well wait up for you as somebody will obviously have to ferry you across to join Melissa."

There was an inflection in the way he said the last
two words which made Thomas look at him sharply.

"Who says I have to join Melissa? I'll stay overnight
on the couch here."

"What a good idea," said Karen relieved before Neville could comment. "That'll save Neville a journey. Are you sure you wouldn't mind, Thomas?"

"I'd prefer it." He sat down on the couch without waiting for a further invitation and crossed his ankles leisurely.

"I'll go and get some blankets," said Karen. "It'll be cold when the fire burns out."

"One'll be enough." After she had left he went over to the phone. "Will Melissa be at the hotel by now, do you think?"

"Presumably," said Neville from the pages of his book. "They left at least half an hour ago."

"You know the hotel number?"

Neville did. Thomas began to make the call and within minutes was speaking to Melissa to tell her he was staying overnight. He had just replaced the receiver when Marney arrived back from the lake and came through into the living-room to join them.

"I must be getting back to the lodge, Neville," he said. "Has Leonie gone to bed? Perhaps you'd thank her again for me for the excellent dinner. Will you be coming over tomorrow?"

"Yes, I suppose so." Neville did not sound enthusiastic at the prospect of resuming his work. "What time do you plan to make a start? I was thinking of driving over at about nine."

"Fine, I'll tell Kelleher. Good night, Thomas."

"So long, Marney, I'll be seeing you."

"Good night, Neville."

"I'll come out and see you off." Neville put aside the book with alacrity and moved out of the room to leave Thomas alone by the flickering flames of the fire.

Thomas picked up the discarded book idly, read a

page and put it down again. He was just trying to find some light music on the radio when Karen returned with some blankets and Neville came back into the house after having seen Marney leave in his jeep.

"I hope you'll be warm enough," Karen was saying as she came into the room. "These are all I could find."

"That'll be fine."

From the distance they heard Neville's footsteps on the stairs as he went up to his bedroom.

"I guess I'm not exactly welcome here," Thomas observed wryly. "He'll find it hard to forgive me for the things he heard me say earlier. I just hope he doesn't take it out on you."

"He'll keep it to himself." She kissed him briefly. "Don't worry, Thomas. I hope you sleep well."

She left him looking guilty and apologetic and went upstairs to join Neville. On her way she glanced in at Snuff. He was still fast asleep, small and peaceful, his thumb trailing at the corner of his mouth, his long lashes shadowing his cheeks.

In the bedroom Neville was undressing; he looked up as she came into the room and closed the door, but did not speak.

Presently she asked: "Did Melissa cause trouble?"

"No, Marney was there to keep the peace. She soon got bored and was relieved when Marney offered to row her back to Kildoun."

"Well, that's something." She decided not to refer to Thomas. Moving across the room she began to wash at the basin, and when she had finished Neville was in bed, a cigarette between his fingers, his eyes watching her intently.

She began to feel uneasy. Perhaps it would be better to mention Thomas after all.

"Thomas and I—" she began but he interrupted her.

"There's no need for you to try to defend him or apologize for him," he said abruptly. "Let's just forget about him for the moment."

She knew she ought to feel relieved at his willingness to dismiss the subject, but she did not. She began to undress. When she came to the bed at last he crushed his cigarette into the ash tray and blew out the light.

"Karen . . ." He had turned to her, pulling her towards him as she slipped between the sheets, and she felt his hard strong body press against her own, his mouth seeking hers in the darkness.

She knew at once that she would have to pretend and so she poured her whole being into acting her part convincingly. If Neville in any way suspected her of being unresponsive he would immediately blame Thomas and accuse him of upsetting her, and whatever happened she was determined that that was something he would never suspect. Afterwards, spent by the effort of deception she lay motionless in Neville's arms, but it was only when he turned and whispered his love for her that she was sure the deception had been successful.

2

The next morning Snuff came pattering into the room soon after seven and woke them by clambering over their feet. He had just settled himself comfortably on

Neville's back when the alarm clock shrilled into life and began to dance angrily across the bedside table.

Neville muttered something bad-tempered, but when the child promptly silenced the clock he opened his eyes and smiled at him without a trace of ill-humor. "Thanks, Snuff. How are you this morning?"

"All right." He slipped off the bed as Neville sat up. "Daddy, can we go for a walk after breakfast?"

"I wish we could, but this morning I have to go back to work. Maybe Aunt Karen would go with you instead."

"Would you, Aunt Karen?"

"Uh-huh. If it's not raining."

"It's not." He pattered over to the window and peered up at the sky. "The clouds are big and high up and moving quickly and the sun's almost shining." He danced over to the door. "I'm going to get dressed."

"Snuff!" called Karen, but he was already out of earshot.

Slipping out of bed she pulled on her robe and went after him to see if he needed any help but he appeared to be self-sufficient. He looked astonished as she came in, as if he considered her intrusion a trespass on his privacy.

"What are you wearing today?" Karen said lightly. "Aren't you going to wear some jeans instead of those little short pants? Then your legs wouldn't get so scratched by the heather."

"They're trousers," said Snuff. "Not pants. And I don't have long ones. Nobody does until they're twelve." He remembered she was a foreigner and added kindly: "It's tradition."

"But I've seen other English boys your age wearing long trousers!"

"Common boys do."

"I beg your pardon?"

"It's common," repeated Snuff, raising his voice. "Common boys wear long trousers at any age. That's tradition too."

"Who said so?"

"Aunt Leonie."

Karen opened her mouth and shut it again. She was conscious not for the first time how difficult her position was in regard to the child. If she openly ridiculed Leonie's snobbishness, it would confuse Snuff and further antagonize Leonie herself if Snuff repeated the criticisms to her.

"Jeans are different from regular long trousers," she said at last. "They can be worn by anyone anywhere. That's tradition too."

"Well, I haven't got any," said Snuff crossly and struggled into a dirty red pullover.

She wanted to tell him to wear a clean one but knew instinctively that he would dislike the idea. Besides, she reflected philosophically, a clean sweater would only end up dirty at the end of the day; why not let him get the dirty sweater dirtier? Resigning herself to be patient she opened the door to go and then glanced back at him.

"It'll be fun to go for a walk together," she said. "I was wondering what to do with myself once your father had gone but now you've solved the problem for me. That was a good idea of yours."

He tried not to look flattered and didn't quite succeed. She was reminded with amusement of Neville.

"Where shall we go?" she asked him. "Shall we walk along to the end of the lake?"

"Okay," he said agreeably, using one of the expressions which his aunt would have detested. "If you like."

"Fine!" She smiled at him. "I'll be looking forward to it." And she stepped out on the landing, closed the door behind her and went downstairs to the kitchen.

Leonie was already dressed and stirring the porridge on the stove. Within a short time of her arrival she had made it clear by her actions that it was she who owned the cottage and she who was responsible for the food and the meals. She also, by means of subtle hints and allusions, had contrived to make Karen feel an interloper.

"I see Thomas stayed the night," she said as Karen entered the kitchen. "I went in to do the fire and found him sprawled on the sofa. It gave me quite a shock."

"It did? I'm sorry—we would have told you but you'd already gone to bed."

"I was wide awake actually," said Leonie. "I can never go to sleep while other people are still up and moving around." She left the words "and making a noise" unsaid but the implication hung in the air with unmistakeable clarity.

"I'll set the table," said Karen, refusing to be drawn into further apologies.

"Would you? Thank you so much. Of course I've no idea what Thomas eats for breakfast."

"You needn't worry about Thomas," Karen said. "He'll be asleep for hours yet."

"I hope not. I wanted to clean that room this morning before I go into Fort William to do some shopping."

"In that case," said Karen with a serenity she was far from feeling, "I'll wake him up and get him his breakfast myself. Please don't worry about it."

She went into the dining-room, set the table briskly to conceal her annoyance and went into the living-room. Thomas was sprawled on the sofa, blankets piled on him from the waist downwards, his chest masked by a snow-white T-shirt.

"Thomas!" Karen shook him mildly. "Wake up."

"Go away, Leonie."

"That's not good enough, Thomas. You know very well it's me. You'll have to get up because Leonie wants to clean the room directly after breakfast."

"Grrr," said Thomas.

She left him, and moving back to the kitchen found Snuff waiting as Leonie filled his bowl with porridge.

"You don't want porridge, do you, Karen?" The implication was that Americans were not capable of appreciating such food.

"Yes, please," said Karen. "Would you like me to cook Neville's eggs and bacon?"

"No, I'll do it. You're on holiday. Besides, I'm used to cooking them."

"I did live with him for nearly two years, you know," said Karen, helping herself to porridge while Snuff poured himself a glass of milk. "I have had experience of cooking his breakfast."

"Well, of course, I didn't mean—"

"Is there toast and marmalade, Aunt?" said Snuff.

"Don't interrupt," said Leonie automatically, but she had already forgotten what she was going to say.

"I'll make you some toast when you've finished your porridge, Snuff," said Karen over her shoulder as she went into the dining-room. "Warm toast tastes nicer than traditional English cold burnt bread."

I must stop, she told herself as she put down her bowl of porridge on the table, I mustn't let her make me angry. To calm herself she went in to look at Thomas. He was, as she had suspected, still asleep.

"Thomas!" She shook him in exasperation. "Thomas!"

"Pas aujourd'hui, cherie," said Thomas distinctly and turned his back.

"You're impossible," retorted Karen, who spoke no French but knew enough to recognize the occasional phrase. "Impossible!" She returned to the dining-room next door, found Snuff already eating with gusto and sat down beside him. Perhaps she would feel less irritated if she had some coffee.

But the pot on the table contained tea.

"Leonie, is there enough water in the kettle for instant coffee?"

"What? Oh no, I'm so sorry, I forgot."

It was obviously going to be one of those mornings.

Presently Neville came down, wearing worn casual clothes and still contriving to look elegant. His presence eased the awkwardness in the atmosphere for a while, but he did not linger long over his breakfast and ten minutes later he was on his way outside to the jeep to begin his first day's work at the plantation.

"I won't be back for lunch, I'm afraid," he said as he kissed Karen goodbye. "Expect me back about six. Will you be all right here alone? Leonie says she's going shopping in Fort William."

"I'll have Snuff with me—and Thomas."

"Well, ring the lodge if anything crops up. There'll

usually be someone there who knows which section of the plantation I'll be working in."

"Fine. But I'll be okay, you don't have to worry."

He smiled, kissed her again and was gone.

She went back to the dining-room to find Leonie clearing away the dishes and Snuff lingering over his last crust of toast and marmalade.

"Is Thomas up yet?" said Leonie, casually stacking two cups together.

"Lord, I'd forgotten him!" She went back into the living-room next door with a mingled feeling of irritation and guilt, and succeeded in waking him, but he was intent on returning to sleep as soon as possible. In the end he grudgingly transferred himself to her bedroom and promptly fell asleep again on the double bed, much to Karen's annoyance.

"Why's he so tired?" inquired Snuff who had been watching the scene with interest from the doorway.

"He's not especially tired, darling. It's just that he's an actor and actors get used to working at night and sleeping in the day. Shall we go out for our walk as soon as I'm dressed? Are you ready?"

"Yes."

"Sure you don't want an extra sweater?"

"No, thank you." He went away politely after she had said she wouldn't be long, and she closed the door after him and began to dress to the accompaniment of her brother's heavy breathing. She put on dark slacks, selected a thick sweater that clung warmly to her body and remembered a scarf for her hair. Her suede walking shoes were still caked with yesterday's mud, but she scraped off the worst of it with a spare nail-file and brushed the pieces out of the window into the flower bed below. When she left the room a minute later she found Snuff sitting on the stairs as he waited for her, and gazing soberly out into space.

"What were you thinking about?" she said lightly, but her words only served to make him shy and he shook his head and went downstairs ahead of her without replying.

Leonie was in the kitchen washing up. She had already declined Karen's offer of help and was now concentrating on her task with an air of efficient martyrdom.

"Snuff and I are going for a walk," Karen said. "I don't know how long we'll be."

"Oh? I'll probably be on my way to Fort William by the time you get back. I'll be home again later this afternoon, I expect. Snuff, you should put on another pullover—it's cold out and it might rain."

"Aunt Karen said I needn't," said Snuff with cunning and had skipped out of the back door in a flash before Leonie could open her mouth to disapprove.

"I asked him if he wanted another sweater," said Karen awkwardly, "but he said he didn't."

"Well, of course," said Leonie with a shrug. "He always does say that." She was very careful not to say: "I know him better than you do" but the implication was obvious. "I hope you have a pleasant walk."

"Thanks," said Karen shortly, and followed Snuff outside into the cool fresh air of the Highland morning. Snuff was already dancing on to the wooden bridge which crossed the stream. He turned to see how far she was behind him, and then danced on again so that he was once more at a distance from her.

"Hey, wait for me!" she protested with a laugh, but he ignored her, and she wondered with a sinking heart how long it would be before she ceased to be a stranger who had left him once and might leave him again, a stranger whom he was determined to keep at arm's length.

He took the path which led west along the shore of the lake, and she followed him at her own pace while he darted to and fro, skipping from side to side and jumping over mud pools. Once when he slowed down for a moment and she came within earshot of him, she heard him humming "Frère Jacques."

"Did you learn that at school, Snuff?"

He nodded, not looking at her, and then saw the tumbled-down ruins to their right by the shore. "What's that place?"

"It's just an old house which nobody has lived in for years. No, Snuff, don't go in there! The walls may not be safe—"

But he had gone and didn't hear her. She followed him with reluctance, remembering how the ruins had reminded her inexplicably of April, and when she reached the doorway, she saw that he was exploring the one large room with excitement.

"There's nothing there, Snuff. Let's go on." Already the smells of damp and decay were making her shiver and she longed to turn back once more into the sunshine.

"Perhaps the people buried their treasure before they left," said Snuff, prodding the soft earth with his toe. "People often did that if they ran away from their homes. Wherever there's a Roman villa they find lots of coins buried in the ground. Monsieur le Professeur says so."

"This isn't a Roman villa, Snuff, just a shack where some poor farmers once tried to make a living. And they didn't run away leaving their money buried—they went away willingly because they had no money and wanted to try to find some elsewhere."

"Oh," said Snuff, not sounding in the least convinced, and went on prodding.

"Come on, let's walk on further. There are plenty of other things to see, and we might come to some better ruins later. This part of the country is full of them."

"Why?" said Snuff. "Why did everyone go away?"

They walked on back to the path while Karen began to explain what little she knew of Highland economics and social history, and presently they were some way from the ruined house and she was able to relax again.

They walked for another half hour and still did not reach the tip of the lake which had seemed deceptively close at hand. The path had become much muddier, and at length Karen decided to turn back. They were within sight of the ruins once more when Snuff asked if they could rest for a few minutes and Karen, agreeing, seated herself on a slab of rock and looked out across the lake to the hotel at Kildoun and the road running past it on the other side of the water.

Snuff began to wander off idly in the direction of the ruins and Karen, restraining her first impulse to call him back, pretended not to notice. After all, she reasoned, if he wanted to look for buried treasure, why should she spoil his fun? She settled herself into a more comfortable position on the rock and went on watching the changing hues of the lake, but when he had not returned after five minutes she got up and went over to the ruins to see what he was doing.

She found him on his hands and knees, scraping at the soft damp earth in one corner of the house with a sharp piece of slate.

"Snuff, what are you doing?" Despite herself, her voice held an echo of uneasiness. It was dark in the ruins and again she felt conscious of her acute dislike of the place.

"I found some treasure," said Snuff complacently, and went on scraping.

"That's not possible, darling," she said sharply. "It's just some old stone embedded in the ground." Still she could not bring herself to step forward across the threshold. And then suddenly her spine was tingling and the panic began to crawl down the back of her neck.

"No, it's not a stone," said Snuff triumphantly. "It's a suitcase. Look! Can you see? Do you think they put jewels in it, or will it just be gold coins?"

There was a silence. Karen was rigid with the full force of appalling suspicions. Movement, even speech, was impossible.

"Here's the other clasp," said Snuff, still scraping patiently. "Now I can open it and see what's inside."

"No!" Her cry startled him so much that he jumped to his feet. Scarcely knowing what she was doing she moved across to him and saw the top of the old suitcase he had unearthed, the clasps rusty and clogged with mud.

"Snuff darling, can you go outside for a moment? Please—just for a moment."

He stared at her, recognizing her distress but puzzled

about its cause. At last he said kindly: "Don't be frightened, it's probably only gold coins. You can look the other way, if you like, while I open it."

"Snuff, please—" But she was too late. He had already pulled back the clasps using all his strength to overcome the rust and mud, and while she watched, too horrified to stop him, he heaved open the lid.

A smell of rotting material floated up to meet them, the damp of mildew and decay.

"Well!" said Snuff in disgust. "Look at that! I thought there would at least be gold coins, but all that's there is a lady's clothes! I wonder who they belong to."

3

Afterwards Karen wondered why she had not felt dizzy with the shock, but all she was conscious of at the time was a feeling of dreadful clarity, as if she had faced an intricate puzzle for a long while only to have the mystery solved when she least expected it. As Snuff turned to her, his baffled annoyance showing clearly in his eyes, she felt herself move over to him and gently draw him to one side so that she could examine the open suitcase more closely.

A garment made out of a material which had once been green lay on top. Resolutely repressing her distaste for handling the mildewed cloth she picked it up and recognized the smart green sheath dress April had worn during her last visit to London. Beneath it were articles of underwear, the lace rotted away, the nylon discolored. A small woodlouse burrowed furtively out of sight as it was so unexpectedly exposed to the sight of day.

"Ugh!" said Snuff. "Creepy-crawly."

"I expect the suitcase is full of them—these clothes won't be any use to anyone now." She scarcely noticed what she said. April, she knew, had had two suitcases. Could the other one be buried here as well? She began to glance swiftly at the damp earth nearby.

"Let's go and tell someone about it," said Snuff. "Will Daddy be back from the plantation soon? Let's tell Daddy."

"No," said Karen abruptly, "we won't tell anyone just yet. Let's make it a secret between the two of us until I find out who the clothes belong to."

Snuff looked pleased at the idea of a secret and then chagrined that he could not boast of his buried treasure.

"Well, it wasn't much of a treasure anyway," he said aloud, consoling himself. "Just a lot of old clothes."

"Then it's a secret between the two of us for the time being," said Karen.

"Okay."

He wandered to the door of the hut and she followed him outside reluctantly, not sure what she should do but knowing only that she wanted a chance to be alone in the ruins for a while. Fortunately the problem was solved for her when Snuff danced back to the path and raced uphill to examine an outcrop of rock. The treasure had apparently lost interest for him.

"I'll follow you more slowly," she called after him. "When you get back to the house see if Uncle Thomas is awake."

That would give him something to do.

He waved to show that he had heard, and when he had disappeared among the rocks she went back again into the ruins. The chill of the place struck her anew as she re-entered it. She shook herself determinedly, and going back to the suitcase, she replaced the dress, drew down the lid and began to scrape back the earth to cover it again. When this was done she found a sharp stick outside and began to prod carefully in the area nearby. She found the second suitcase less than three minutes later. It was buried in another shallow grave, and without much difficulty she unearthed one corner, just to prove to herself that she was not mistaken.

After that she went outside, walked a little way from the ruins and sat down calmly on a rock to gaze out over the lake before her.

Suddenly she began to tremble. April's two suitcases were buried here near the house! And obviously it hadn't been April who had done the burying. April had almost certainly never left the house that morning. She was dead, and someone . . . someone had buried the suitcases to create the illusion that she had left safely, someone had towed the boat across the lake to hint at her escape route, someone had disposed of the body.

Her thoughts raced on with frightening speed. Why had the suitcases been buried and not thrown in the lake? Because they might have been discovered by fishermen fishing in the clear waters in high summer, or by sportsmen shooting wild duck in the rushes which fringed the lake below Kildoun. But no one was going to go digging in ruins long forgotten. No one except a child bent on finding buried treasure.

Buried. Buried in a grave.

Karen thought of her sister for one long icy moment of fear. If April was dead, where was the body? Perhaps the ruins . . . But no, that couldn't be. Putrefied flesh stank. A shallow grave wouldn't have been able to contain the smell.

She felt she was going to be sick. She got up hurriedly and stumbled back to the path, and presently the feeling of nausea passed, leaving her feeling weak and shaken. She did not know what to do. She was convinced now that April had been murdered, but when she tried to consider who had killed her and concealed both crime and victim with such hideous efficiency, her mind shied away from the possible suspects confronting her. Thomas, Leonie, Neville, Marney . . . She forced herself to consider each of them for a long moment. Thomas, she decided, could not be guilty. If he was, he wouldn't be so ready to proclaim that April was murdered (but wasn't he only doing so in an attempt to turn her against Neville?). "Oh nonsense!" she said aloud to herself with a conviction she was far from feeling. "Thomas isn't a murderer." Then there was Leonie. Karen hastily turned from Thomas to a consideration of her sister-in-law. Leonie had loathed April, but one hardly committed murder merely because of loathing (Or did one? People could murder each other for a nickel. Yes, but it wasn't that kind of murder . . . What kind of murder?). Well, thought Karen, never mind Leonie. The next suspect was— well, she wouldn't think of Neville just yet. The last suspect was Marney. Could Marney conceivably be a murderer? Marney with his gentleness, his courtesy, his old-fashioned charm . . . "But he had the brain to commit the crime," she told herself stubbornly. "Or rather, to cover up the crime. And whoever covered up the crime was no fool. Everything was remembered, even the last detail of leaving a boat on the Kildoun side of the lake to create the illusion that April had rowed herself across to escape."

Marney had been attracted to April; she could remember noticing three years ago in London how April had affected Marney when they had first met. Karen had thought little of it at the time because she was so used to seeing the effect which April had on men, but now she began to wonder. Supposing Marney had become involved with April. Supposing . . . But Neville had been the one involved with April, not Marney. Her thoughts balked again at the thought of Neville's possible guilt, but at last with a feeling of panic she let the possibility sink into her mind.

But no, Neville could not, would not have committed murder. Surely there would have been something to give him away, something which would have enabled her to detect his guilt! She would refuse to believe him guilty. She would not admit it. Nothing would make her admit it.

"But if I tell Thomas about the clothes," she said aloud to herself, "he'll at once believe Neville killed her."

The thought made her rigid with horror. Supposing Melissa should somehow discover about the clothes! It would give her just the lever she needed to strike back at Neville. Whatever happened neither Melissa nor anyone else must find out about the clothes.

But then what was she to do? Live the rest of her life with all her terrible suspicions? Conceal the fact that her sister had been murdered? Besides, it would be useless to expect Snuff to keep quiet forever about his startling find in the ruins. Sooner or later he would forget it was a secret or unwittingly give the game away, and all the details would come out.

She stopped, confusion bringing her to a halt. She did not know what to do, and yet knew that she must do something. And as she stood there, perfectly still, staring across the lake to the mountains beyond, she had the faintest glimmer of an idea.

If she could prove conclusively to herself who had killed April, then at least she would not have to live with her doubts and suspicions. After all, she thought uncertainly, in some ways Thomas had been right when he had said April had got what she deserved. All Karen was concerned to prove was whether or not Neville was guilty. If she managed to prove to herself that Leonie or Marney had killed April, then there was no need for her to resurrect the matter by going to the police. She would let sleeping dogs lie. As long as she knew that Neville was innocent she could come to terms with the situation without difficulty.

A coldness gripped her heart again, making breathing painful. She was revolted by the thought of proving any of the four people guilty of murder, and frightened of what she might discover, but the prospect of living in doubt, of forever wondering what had happened was more horrifying still. Moving very slowly, the expression in her eyes remote and unseeing, she reached the house and raised an unsteady hand to unlatch the back door.

4

Upstairs Thomas was awake and telling a round-eyed Snuff the story of his life. Karen came slowly into the room to ask if he wanted coffee.

"And bacon and eggs," he said, "and toast, please."

"Porridge?"

"You're kidding." He turned again to Snuff. "Well, where was I? Yes, when I was fourteen I went water-skiing . . ."

She left him to his reminiscences and went down to the kitchen. Leonie had evidently left for Fort William, for there was no sign of her. Presently Thomas came downstairs to eat his breakfast while Karen and Snuff had a snack lunch, and later Snuff wandered up the stream again on another of his private expeditions, his sweater bright against the green-brown of the mountainside and the purple of the heather.

The telephone rang just as Thomas was finishing his third cup of coffee. He reached back and grabbed the receiver.

"Hello? Oh hi, Melissa . . ." He made a face at Karen. "Well, I haven't made any plans—I've only just got up . . . Let me call you back in ten minutes." He dropped the receiver hastily back in its cradle.

"What did she want?"

"I don't know—I didn't stay long enough to ask." He gulped down the rest of his coffee. "Why doesn't she go off to her tweed mill?" He stood up, stretched and yawned. "I guess I'll get dressed and maybe try a

bit of fishing up the stream. Do you want to come fishing with me?"

"If I can catch Snuff to tell him where to find us."

Snuff decided to join them and they set off together
about half an hour later after Thomas had assembled
Neville's fishing tackle and gear. The telephone shrilled
angrily again just as they were leaving.

"Don't answer it," said Thomas. "I'll call her when
we get back, but I don't want to talk to her now."

When they returned to the house some time later
Leonie had arrived back from her shopping expedition
and was putting away the provisions in the kitchen.

"I decided not to go to Fort William," she said, "so I
stopped at the general store on the way there to buy the
things we needed most. Melissa rang up, Thomas, and
wanted you to phone back whenever you came in."

"Hell," said Thomas and went moodily into the dining-room to the telephone.

"Thomas," said Karen, following him, "I think I'm
going to walk over to the plantation to the lodge and
meet Neville when he stops work. Leonie's here now to
look after Snuff so you don't have to worry about him.
I'll be coming back with Neville in the jeep around
six."

"I'll come with you," he said instantly, seizing the
opportunity to avoid Melissa.

"No," said Karen firmly. "You call Melissa and find
out what she wants. After all, she did give you a free
ride up here, don't forget. You owe her something."

Thomas didn't seem to think so, but after a few
minutes' wrangling he ungraciously picked up the receiver. Leaving him glaring after her, Karen went into

the kitchen to tell Leonie where she was going and then paused to say goodbye to Snuff before going outside once more into the cool air of late afternoon.

Outside she crossed the stream by the wooden footbridge, and began the walk up the rough track which led uphill to the pass. The climb was steep. Several times she had to pause to get her breath, and as she turned to look back over the way she had come she was impressed afresh by the magnificence of the scenery, the lake ringed by hills, the hills hemmed in by mountains, the varying shades of the moors as the sun appeared and disappeared behind enormous banks of cloud.

It was lonely. There was not another living thing in sight. Swiftly she walked on uphill and at last reached the pass and stood between the twin shoulders of the mountain to gaze into the next valley, to the dark silent acres of Plantation Q.

It began to rain as she walked downhill, a light Highland drizzle, but before she could concern herself about getting wet it had stopped and the track had straightened out to follow the cut through the trees. The conifers were on all sides of her now, their dark boughs shoulder to shoulder, the ground beneath them a grave of pine needles. The silence was immense, unnerving. There seemed to be no birds singing or calling to one another, and there was no wind to sigh through the branches. Karen quickened her pace instinctively, and then at last the trees ended as abruptly as they had begun and she saw the mellow red brick of the lodge with the barn nearby which housed the fleet of foresters' jeeps.

The cook, an old Highland woman who had never

been further south than Edinburgh, saw her through the window, gave her a toothless smile and told her that Neville was still out on the plantation.

Karen had guessed as much; on reaching the front of the house she went through the open front door into the hall and immediately met one of the young foresters who repeated the cook's information.

"Dr. West's here, though," he told her helpfully. "He's working in his office—second door on the right."

She felt reluctant to disturb Marney, but then realized with an even greater reluctance that here was an ideal opportunity to see him alone and encourage him to talk of the past. Summoning her determination she knocked softly on the door, opened it and went through into the room.

His smile seemed to be genuine enough. "Karen!" He rose to his feet. "Well, this is a surprise. I suppose you walked over? Do sit down."

He began to clear some files off one of the chairs.

"I don't want to interrupt you—"

"No, that's all right. I'm almost finished. Would you like some tea after your walk?"

"No, but if there's a glass of water . . ."

He brought it instantly from the kitchen and sat down again behind his desk as she drank it.

"I'd forgotten how long it takes to walk over," she said between sips, "and what an uphill climb it is to the pass."

"I hope you don't intend to walk back!"

"No!" she agreed ruefully. "I'll wait for Neville. Whereabouts on the plantation is he?"

"Somewhere out in section five. Would you like me to drive out there to find him?"

"Oh no—no, I mustn't interrupt him—"

"They're planting new seedlings out there . . ." He began to tell her about the trees with a curious zest, and described how an experiment in planting them in a certain area of the plantation had failed. "The ground was too rocky," he said. "I advised from the beginning that they would be better off in section five. Section five has a good sub-soil—it's further from the rocky slopes of the mountain, closer to the floor of the valley."

The image of planting the seedlings in soft earth reminded her of the suitcases buried in their shallow graves. She put down her glass of water, and fumbled for a cigarette.

"I'm sorry," said Marney suddenly. "I must stop talking shop. I'm sure you're not interested in all these details about the trees."

She inhaled from her cigarette, shook out the match slowly. "It's odd to be back here again at Plantation Q," she said, "and hearing you talk about the trees." She glanced around the room. "Of course last time I was here I couldn't have cared less what anyone was talking about."

There was a pause. Then: "No," said Marney awkwardly. "I suppose not."

She pretended to think that he did not remember the occasion of her last visit to Plantation Q. "I ended up here the day I found Neville and April at the house," she said baldly. "I rushed out stupidly without thinking and got lost on the plantation for hours before Neville found me within half a mile of the lodge and brought me here—I expect he told you about it afterwards."

"He mentioned it, yes." Marney's voice was strained.

"The funny thing is that I don't recall seeing you at

all, but you were at the lodge then, weren't you? Or were you out on the plantation at the time?"

"Yes, I was out all morning working on my own about three miles from here. I became so absorbed in my work that I didn't even drive back to the lodge for lunch till nearly two. That was why I didn't see you or learn what had been going on until it was all over. Thomas fetched you from the lodge, didn't he? I think I got back soon after he had taken you away. Neville was in a frightful state and I gave him a whisky and tried to calm him down before driving him back to the house. We left Scotland that same afternoon, I remember—my work was completed by then and Neville decided to dash back to London after you. He never caught up with you, did he? You got on a plane to New York and that was that . . . I'm sorry, I'm digressing unnecessarily. Forgive me."

"No—no, that's all right. Leonie was there when Neville got back to the house with you presumably."

"Yes, Leonie was waiting for us, and—no, Snuff wasn't there, of course. I was forgetting."

"I'd left him in London with a cousin of his mother's. Was Neville surprised to find April had gone?"

"Yes, he immediately asked Leonie where she was and Leonie said she had assumed April was with him. After that they went upstairs to look for her and found her clothes and suitcases were gone—and so had one of the boats from the jetty. Leonie said she supposed April must have left just before she had arrived back at the house from the lodge at eleven that morning."

Marney looked guilty. "You know, I felt very badly about that afterwards. Leonie had telephoned me the night before from the house soon after April's arrival, and said she wanted to see me as soon as possible. Since it was late I suggested she come over to the lodge the following morning but . . . well, when I woke up the next morning I completely forgot I'd arranged to meet her at the lodge at ten. The trouble was that I had had a most absorbing talk with Kelleher at breakfast about my project and I was so anxious to get to work that the thought of Leonie simply didn't enter my head. I felt very embarrassed later when I returned to the lodge and found the note she had left me."

"She left you a note?"

"Yes, it was all about Neville's behavior in suggesting April come to the farm while Leonie was on holiday there. I know Neville swore there was no rendezvous, but not unnaturally Leonie found it hard to believe him. She was furious. I think she'd come to see me to seek moral support before she asked Neville to leave."

"Was that the first you knew of April being at the farm?"

"No, I knew April was there before I heard from Leonie that she too was at the farm. Before Leonie spoke to me on the phone that evening—the evening April arrived—I rang up the house to have a word with Neville and he told me then what had happened. He didn't say much, just that it was all awkward, that April was there, and he couldn't talk for more than a moment. He didn't mention Leonie at all." He made a grimace of distaste. "As soon as he told me April was there I wished he hadn't mentioned it. Naturally I thought they were alone at the farm together, and the knowledge made me feel shabby, as if I was somehow helping him to be unfaithful to you simply by knowing what he was doing. Even when I found out Leonie was there too I still felt guilty. To be very frank, Karen, I think Neville got out of that corner much more easily than he deserved. April might have given him a lot of trouble. I'm only surprised he didn't have more difficulty in getting rid of her."

"I think he had a huge row with her before he left the house to look for me—"

"All the more reason why she should want to make trouble for him afterwards." He stood up abruptly and walked over to the window, his hands thrust deep in the pockets of his worn corduroys. "Neville says he's never heard from her since."

"No." She decided to change the subject quickly in case he was on the brink of bringing up the possibility of April's death, accidental or otherwise. "Talking of Neville, Marney—"

"Yes, are you sure you wouldn't like me to drive you out to section five? He should still be there."

"Well, perhaps if it's not too much trouble—"

"No, I'd like some fresh air."

He put on an old tweed jacket, locked away his papers and took her outside. Rain was falling lightly again, but there was blue sky in the west and the shower was already half over. There was a jeep in the barn, and after Marney had helped Karen inside he sat down behind the wheel and started the engine. A moment later they were driving away from the lodge and swinging into a wide cut which led westward parallel to the mountain slopes.

After ten minutes of rough driving they reached another cut and beyond it lay a forest of little trees no more than two feet high. Bordering this plantation of embryos was a muddled section where trees had been felled and the ground ploughed up. Among the furrows the earth shone black as pitch in the clear afternoon light.

Neville and a group of men appeared to be bent over a fallen tree. Karen wondered what they were doing and marveled idly at the complexity of a subject which she would have thought so simple. She would not have imagined that trees could assume such importance that one small fallen conifer could hold the interest of six men. "What are they doing?" she asked Marney automatically.

"I don't know. Perhaps there's some malformation of the roots."

Neville had seen them and was waving his arm in greeting. Marney halted the jeep.

"Trouble, Neville?"

"No, just a minor puzzle. It seems there's granite nearer the surface here than we thought . . ." He went on talking, speaking competently in technicalities, but Karen didn't hear him. She heard nothing at all. Her whole mind was suddenly focused on the little fallen conifer and the hole in the ground where its roots had been. An idea filled her mind, chilling her spine and prickling her scalp. No wonder April's body had never been found. The murderer had never thrown it in the lake at all, never tried to bury it in the rough ground near the farm. April's body was somewhere on this side of the mountains, somewhere in the black earth of Plantation Q.

Six

1

Reason and logic succeeded her panic less than a minute later, but Karen was still aware of feeling shaken. The idea that April's body lay buried somewhere on Plantation Q was a mere quirk of her mind, she decided, a sequel to the events of the morning when she had found the suitcases in their shallow graves. Now she was imagining possible graves everywhere without any substantiating evidence whatsoever. She was fast allowing her nerves to get the better of her; it was time she pulled herself together and ceased to give full rein to her imagination.

But her tenseness persisted. Marney was out in a jeep that morning, she found herself thinking; he was all alone in a remote section of the plantation; he could have driven over to the farm, killed April and driven the body back to the plantation for burial. Or perhaps Neville . . . no, Neville and April must have approached the house by hired boat from the lake the night before because when Karen had arrived the following morning there had been no sign of any jeep parked by the croft. But where had Neville been during the morning of April's disappearance? She only had his word that he had spent three hours looking for her; he could have walked to the lodge in three quarters of an hour, taken one of the fleet of jeeps, driven back, killed April and removed the body . . . For that matter Leonie could have done the same thing; it was a fact that she had walked over to the lodge that morning; she could have taken a jeep from the barn; by the time she had arrived for her ten o'clock rendezvous with Marney everyone would have been at work on the plantation and the lodge would have been deserted save for the deaf old Highland cook in the kitchens . . .

"Are you all right?" she heard Neville say suddenly. "You're very quiet."

"Yes, I'm fine. Just a little tired." Karen resolutely tried to close her mind against the past and concentrate on the present before Neville became more suspicious and asked further questions. They had left the lodge by this time after saying goodbye to Marney and the foresters. Neville was coaxing his jeep uphill on their way back to the farm in the next valley, and as they reached the pass Karen made a great effort to become entirely absorbed in the scenery once more. But the effort was useless. Still she could think only of a hidden grave somewhere beneath dark firs, the soft black earth concealed by pine needles and protected by the regulations covering the plantation.

"Neville."

His eyes continued to watch the rough track as he concentrated on the task of driving. "Yes?"

"How often are the trees cut down and the ground ploughed up?"

He laughed. "Darling, forestry isn't quite so simple as that! There's no clear-cut answer. Why?"

"I was just wondering. No special reason."

They began the descent into the valley. Far below them lay the lake, its waters still and calm, the surrounding hills mellow in the evening light. Suddenly without warning Neville halted the jeep and switched off the engine.

"What's the matter, darling?" he said casually, turning to face her. "I hope you're not worrying in case April fell into a furrow on Plantation Q and obligingly buried herself afterwards."

His perception both frightened her and took her breath away. "I thought we'd agreed to forget April?" she heard herself say automatically.

"I thought so too," he said, "but I can see you're thinking about her all the time—wondering if there was anything in what Melissa said—"

"No, Neville!" Yet she was unnerved by his betrayal that he too had been thinking of April and worrying about Melissa's malice.

"Well, in case you were wondering about the plantation—"

"I wasn't."

"No? Well, why—"

"Neville, let's drive on and not discuss it any further. I'm tired, and I'm sure you are too, and I want to get home."

He did not answer, but glanced aside at the lake in the distance. His mouth was a hard line, his eyes sullen. Presently he said: "I wasn't wholly honest with you the other night when we first discussed April's disappearance. For a long time now I've been wondering if she was dead, but I didn't see how she could be. Suicide was out of the question, and if she had had an accident the body would have been found eventually, no matter where it was, and you would have been traced and notified. Eventually I considered the possibility of murder and put it aside as being too far-fetched, but when Melissa made her bloody insinuations I considered the possibility again. It still seemed unlikely, but after thinking very carefully I could see one could make out a case for saying it was unlikely that April had ever left this area. And if she had never left this area and her body had been deliberately hidden, that meant without a doubt that she had been murdered." He was fumbling for a cigarette. After a moment he found a packet and struck a match. Then: "Well, of course I considered the plantation," he said. "In some ways it presents a better place for a grave than the ground around the house which is stony and hard. The murderer would have wanted to dig a grave as quickly as possible, but to dig a grave near the house would have taken some time and a lot of effort."

Karen thought in a flash of the soft floor of the ruined house, but she remained silent, waiting for him to go on. "The Plantation has a hard stony soil in some areas," he was saying, "but there are also areas where the earth is soft and pliable. If the murderer knew where to dig he could conceal the body quickly in a place no bull-dozer would ever disturb."

It suddenly seemed very cold. Karen shivered. "If the murderer knew where to dig . . ."

"Exactly." He shrugged with impatience. "But the proposition that April's buried in the plantation is untenable anyway because of the problem of transportation. No murderer would walk from the farm up the mountain to the pass and into the next valley with his victim's body under one arm and a spade under the other, and there was no jeep. I had only arrived at the house the night before—three hours before April—and I had come across the lake, not over the hills by jeep from Plantation Q."

"Then where's April buried?"

"I've no idea, but I know this. If we could find April's grave I think we'd have a good idea who killed her. But until we find the grave there's no concrete evidence that she's dead and not merely missing."

Karen shivered again. "Do you—is there anyone who—" But her voice refused to put the question into words.

"Is there anyone whom I suspect of murder? Well, frankly, no." He laughed shortly, without mirth. "As far as I can see we two are the only ones who had any motive for murdering her, and I know as sure as hell that I didn't and as I can't quite visualize you killing a butterfly, let alone your own twin sister, that hypothesis doesn't seem very convincing to me."

The notion that she herself could be considered a suspect for the crime so appalled her that for a moment she could not reply. Then: "I guess the police might suspect me, if they knew about it," she said panic-stricken. "I could have pretended to be lost on the plantation. After shaking you off my trail I could have crept back to the house, killed her—"

"Rubbish," said Neville. "For one thing you didn't know I was going to rush out after you after wasting ten minutes quarreling with April. You didn't even know I was trying to find you until I finally discovered you half a mile from the lodge three hours later. I saw you enter the woods of the plantation when I reached the pass, but you never looked back. So if you decided to kill April, how did you know she'd be alone at the farm without me to protect her? Also, if you were going to kill her—how fantastic it sounds even to put such a theory into words!—you'd have killed her in a rage on discovering her with me. You would never have summoned up the will to kill her once your anger had cooled. Then again we come back to this problem of the corpse. If you killed April what did you do with her afterwards? I don't believe you'd be cold-blooded enough to work out all those details covering up the murder—you didn't hate April enough for that. I think if you'd killed her you'd have simply phoned the police and confessed."

She smiled in spite of herself. "In other words you think I'd be a bad murderer!"

"I don't think you'd have either the physical or emotional stamina to run backwards and forwards between the house and the plantation, kill April, dispose of the body, tow the spare boat across the lake, and run back to the plantation in time to be discovered by me half a mile from the lodge! The idea's absurd and I think the police would be the first to admit it."

She was vaguely aware of relief but such was her tension that it made little impression on her. After a moment she said unsteadily: "Neville, what did April say when you quarrleed with her? Was it a very bad quarrel?"

His eyes were dark and withdrawn. He glanced at her, then glanced away. "It was unpleasant. I don't remember it clearly."

"Did she—"

"Oh yes, she stormed, raged, threatened, screamed —thank God we were alone and there was no one else within earshot! In a way the quarrel was my fault. I was so appalled that you should have come upon us like that, so shattered at the realization of what you must have been thinking. It was as if someone had slapped me across the face and woken me up in the most unpleasant way possible. I said a few curt words to April, telling her she'd better start to pack her things, and she immediately flared up—it all happened so quickly. Within seconds she was accusing me of all manner of things, and as I thought that was merely a case of the pot calling the kettle black, I was stung into replying . . . Then she started accusing you. When I saw how much she hated you, I—"

"She was always jealous. I tried to make it up to her so many times but she wouldn't let me."

"Yes, so she said. She laughed and said how she despised you."

"What did you say to that?"

"I hit her," said Neville.

She stared at him in disbelief. She saw his mouth twist in a wry smile.

"I have to admit I wasn't acting like a true English gentleman at that stage of the proceedings."

"But—"

"Of course, I shouldn't have hit her but I was so furious at the thought of what she had done, so furious with myself—the whole situation." He shrugged. "I hit her across the mouth, and she flew at me like a wildcat, clawing and screaming. I pushed her aside, and she overbalanced and fell to the floor. While she was picking herself up I walked out of the house and set off to try to find you."

"And—and you never saw her again."

He looked at her. His face, she noticed for the first time, was very white. "No," he said, "no, I swear to you, Karen, that I never saw her again. And when I last saw her she was alive."

2

The clouds had drifted inland to leave the mountains silhouetted against the clear summer sky, and the lake was a slim blue mirror on the floor of the valley. Even though it was after six by the time the jeep reached the farm the light had not yet turned golden, and Karen was reminded of how far north this land was and how short the nights were in consequence.

Neville halted the jeep, helped her to dismount and walked with her across the burn and past the rockery to the back door. In the kitchen a variety of pots simmered on the stove, but there was no one about. Karen went through into the hall and almost at once heard Snuff's clear treble say querulously:

"But it was a very disappointing treasure. Just a lot of lady's clothes."

My God, thought Karen, jerked to a standstill. She

could feel the color drain from her face with the shock.

Neville bumped into her. "What's the matter?"

She could not answer.

"Neville?" called Leonie's voice from the living-room and the next moment she was confronting them in the hall. "Thank God you're back!" she exclaimed with relief. "Snuff has been telling us the most extraordinary stories . . ." Her voice trailed off as she darted a highly suspicious glance in Karen's direction.

The color flooded back to Karen's face as suddenly as it had left it. To her helplessness and fury she felt her cheeks burn scarlet. Neville wheeled round to face her. "What's this?"

"I—" Karen began faintly but Leonie interrupted her.

"Snuff says he discovered two suitcases full of women's clothes buried beneath the floor of the ruined house—"

"What!" Neville stared at her. Then: "Where is he?" He pushed past her. "Let me talk to him. He must be making it up."

"He says Karen told him to say nothing."

There was a short, electric silence. Karen found herself speechless, unable to meet either Neville's or Leonie's eyes. And then somewhere far away Melissa's voice, low and indolent, drawled: "But Snuff darling, why did Aunt Karen ask you to keep it a secret?"

Neville moved involuntarily. "What's Melissa doing here?"

"Don't ask me," said Leonie in a tone which indicated she couldn't possibly be held responsible. "Thomas brought her over here this afternoon."

Neville without a word went past her into the living-room, and Karen, not wanting to be left alone with Leonie, followed him automatically.

Snuff was sitting on the floor with his story-book, and on his face was a cross expression which seemed to suggest that he wished all adults would go away and leave him alone. In one of the armchairs sat Melissa, faultlessly elegant, noticeably undistrubed by Neville's arrival.

"What are you doing here?" said Neville abruptly, and her eyebrows raised themselves in disapproval of his tone of voice.

"Thomas took me for a row on the lake and then when it came on to rain I suggested we shelter at the cottage," she answered unruffled. "It was a heavy squall and the cottage was close at hand . . . I must say, darling, you're not exactly the perfect host this evening."

"Where's Thomas?"

"He's gone down to the ruined house," said Melissa, "to confirm Snuff's tales of buried treasure."

"Neville—" Leonie began.

"It wasn't treasure!" Snuff objected aggressively. "Just a lot of old clothes!"

"Snuff!" said Leonie sharply. "You sounded very rude—how dare you speak like that!"

"Aunt Karen didn't say it was rude," said Snuff nastily, and began to scramble to his feet to make his escape, his story-book tucked tightly under one arm.

"Never mind what Aunt Karen didn't say! Apologize to Aunt Melissa at once."

"She's not my aunt."

"Snuff—"

But he took no notice. Karen suddenly realized he

was standing before her, looking up at her in fury. "I didn't mean to tell," he said aggrieved. "But I said something I didn't mean to say and they went on and on and on at me—"

"It's all right, Snuff. I understand."

"It's all right, Snuff," said Neville kindly, stooping to comfort him. "It doesn't matter. Nobody's cross with you." He glanced at Karen abruptly. "What on earth's this all about?"

All eyes were upon her. She struggled to pull herself together, to talk in a normal tone of voice. "I—I went for a walk with Snuff. He found—accidentally—in the ruined house—"

"Two suitcases of women's clothes," said Leonie crisply. "Buried under the floor."

"Why didn't you tell me about it?" Neville said at once to Karen. "Why did you say nothing?"

"I—I wanted to think—"

He turned and strode over to the front porch. "I'm going to join Thomas."

"So you said nothing," said Leonie disapprovingly to Karen as the front door slammed. "What a foolish thing to do."

Karen was stung to defend herself. "What do you suggest I should have done?" she flared. "Phoned the police?"

"Well, you might at least have told me. After all, I was here three years ago when—and you should have told Neville too, of course."

"I think she should have called the police," drawled Melissa from the hearth. "If they're April's clothes I think it proves pretty conclusively what happened to April."

Leonie was incensed. "Are you suggesting—"

"You ask your sister-in-law again why she didn't tell her husband about her little find! Ask her if she wasn't worried that she'd just become reconciled to a murderer!"

"How *dare* you!" Leonie's face was crimson. "How dare you insinuate such things about my brother!" She turned to Karen. "How can you stand there and let her say such things?"

"I—"

But Leonie had turned back to Melissa. "Please leave my house at once—this instant! I never invited you here anyway. Go on—get out! I never want to see you again."

"Dear me," said Melissa, "how dramatic." She began to draw on her beautiful leather gloves carefully, smoothing the material over each finger. "And who, pray, is going to row me across the lake? Or am I supposed to swim?"

"Row yourself over," said Leonie, and trembling with rage stalked out of the room to the kitchen. The door slammed after her with a force that shook the house.

Snuff was round-eyed. Karen stooped over him and took his hand in hers. "I think if you want to read in peace, darling, you'll have to read upstairs. Shall I come with you?"

"No, thank you," said Snuff, withdrawing his hand with dignity, and walked away without looking back.

Something seemed to twist beneath Karen's heart as she watched him go. She longed to be able to reach him, but knew that the barriers he had raised to reject the adult world were at that moment insuperable.

"My dear," said Melissa, smoothing her hands over her hips and glancing at herself in the mirror. *"What a scene."*

Karen did not answer her. She did not trust herself to speak.

Her feet carried her across the hall again and she found herself opening the front door and stepping out into the cool air of early evening. After taking a deep breath to steady herself, she set off towards the ruined house beyond the stream and less than three minutes later had reached the crumbling walls.

Neville and Thomas were stooped over the two suitcases which lay excavated amidst the upheaval of dark earth, but as they heard her approach they straightened their backs and turned to look at her.

"Karen," said Thomas soberly, wiping the sweat off his forehead with the back of his hand, "you should have told us."

"I—I know . . ." She leant against the doorway suddenly in exhaustion and closed her eyes. As if from a long way away she heard herself say: "I was too shocked—too dazed—I just wanted to think." And then all at once Neville's arms were around her and holding her close to him, and Neville's voice was saying softly: "I understand."

She opened her eyes gratefully and saw his face inches from her own. There was compassion in his eyes but also something else, a hint of wariness, or reserve, of speculation.

"Maybe we ought to dig up this whole floor, Neville," Thomas was saying. "Do you reckon anything else could be buried here besides the suitcases?"

"I doubt it. We can try digging, I suppose, but I'd be

surprised if we found anything. The suitcases take up most of the soft ground here—you can see that over there by the wall the granite is showing beneath the weeds. If you were to take a sharp stick and poke around I think you'd strike rock close to the surface except in this section where the suitcases were buried."

"Where can I find a sharp stick?"

"I believe there are stakes for sweet peas and runner beans in Leonie's gardening shed by the house, if you want to get one. I'm going to take Karen back to the house."

"Thomas," said Karen, "I wish you'd row Melissa back to Kildoun. Leonie has just ordered her out of the house but she won't go for lack of transport."

Thomas made a rude comment about what Melissa could do with herself and began stabbing the earth savagely with the sharp edge of the spade.

"You've got the hell of a nerve to say that," said Neville annoyed. "If it hadn't been for you she wouldn't be here now."

"Please!" said Karen in despair. "Don't you two quarrel as well! That would be more than I could bear!"

"I think we ought to have some sort of conference to decide what should be done," said Neville. "Perhaps we'd better not get rid of Melissa until we've agreed on some course of action. Why don't you come back with us now, Thomas? I doubt if you'll find anything else here, but if you're not satisfied you can come back and search again later."

"Thanks," said Thomas curtly. "I will." He left the spade leaning against the wall and followed them outside with reluctance.

They returned to the house in silence. Karen was conscious of a sense of approaching disaster. Now what would happen? Would someone call the police? But there was still no body, no proof of murder. She shuddered violently, the wave of revulsion shaking her through and through, and glanced at Neville, but he was staring straight ahead, his face expressionless, his hands tight fists in the pockets of his trousers. She wondered what he was thinking.

They reached the house.

"Leonie?" called Neville abruptly as he entered the hall.

There were footsteps in the kitchen; the door opened. "Ah there you are, Thomas," said Leonie, looking past her brother and glimpsing Thomas on the porch. "Could you kindly row your friend back to Kildoun as soon as possible? This is my house and I'm becoming a little tired of uninvited guests."

"Before Melissa goes," said Neville abruptly, "we have to decide what should be done about Snuff's 'treasure.' Could you come into the living-room a moment?"

Leonie looked as if the last thing she wanted to do was to breathe the same air that Melissa breathed, but she gave in with bad grace and followed them through the small dining-room into the living-room beyond. Melissa had mixed herself a drink and was standing by the window; from the radio came the sound of an interview, a discussion of the approaching Edinburgh Festival. Neville turned the switch; the radio died and silence fell upon the room.

"It seems the suitcases are April's without a doubt,"

he said to Melissa. "Both Thomas and I were fully agreed on that."

"But of course!" said Melissa ironically. "Did you really expect them to be anyone else's? I've said all along that she was murdered, and this merely confirms my suspicions."

"Seeing you're so smart, honey," said Thomas, "maybe you can tell us where the body's buried? It might save us a lot of waltzing around if you could exercise your clairvoyant talents in that direction."

Melissa seemed impervious to sarcasm. She shrugged her shoulders. "How should I know? I wasn't even here three years ago. Why not ask someone who was?"

"Neville," said Leonie. "The ruined house—"

"No, I'm fairly certain there's nothing else there except the suitcases although Thomas is going to have another look later."

"Then where—" Leonie broke off, the question unphrased.

"I don't know," said Neville. "I don't know where the body can be."

"How about Plantation Q, darling?" said Melissa. "That would be a good burial ground, wouldn't it? Very convenient for anyone who knew their way around there well."

Leonie and Karen began to speak together. In the pause while they each broke off and waited for the other to speak, Neville said: "Whether she's buried on the plantation or not, there's a chance that the body may never be found. The question at the moment is not where the body is but what we should do—if anything —about the discovery of the suitcases."

Leonie said rapidly: "I suppose there's no chance of it being some sort of accident? There's no possibility—"

"None, as I see it," said Neville flatly. "Someone deliberately created the impression that April had packed her bags, left the farm and rowed over the lake—the impression that April had left alive. Why should April herself bury her suitcases and leave without her belongings?"

There was an awkward silence which began to lengthen unbearably. Karen felt her heart bumping fast against her ribs, her nails digging into the palms of her hands.

"Well," said Melissa, "to be quite frank, I think the police should be informed. It's obvious that there's been some sort of foul play."

"But nothing can be proved," said Neville. "Even if the body is found they'll probably still be unable to prove anything. All it will mean is that the five of us who had access to the house at the time, and who therefore come under suspicion, will be questioned and cross-questioned by the police and caused endless unpleasantness."

"Well, why shouldn't you be?" said Melissa coolly. "It's obvious that one of you is a murderer."

"But what of the four who are innocent?" demanded Thomas. "Besides, personally I think that whoever killed April did more than one person a good turn."

Leonie opened her mouth to protest automatically against this condonation of murder, but only succeeded in looking as if she agreed with what he had said. Then: "How can you be sure, Neville, that one of us

five . . . I don't understand. Perhaps one of the foresters went berserk—perhaps one of them came over to
see her, attacked her for some reason—"

"I doubt if anyone who went berserk like that could
have covered up the crime so efficiently afterwards, and
anyway no one at Plantation Q except Marney knew
April was. here. I didn't advertise her presence to all
and sundry. Also, how could anyone not familiar with
the farm or this side of the mountain have known
where to find April's clothes and where to bury the
suitcases quickly in soft ground? It's out of the question."

"Marney should know about all this," said Leonie
suddenly. "Let me ring him up and ask him to come
over."

"No, wait," said Neville. "Let's first decide what
we're going to do. Normally I would favor going to the
police, but at this stage I can't see what such a move
would achieve apart from engulfing us all in notoriety
in the press and putting each one of us through a hell
of inquisition—to no avail."

"What fine advice," said Melissa, "from such an up-
standing pillar of society and a senior member of the
civil service."

"Melissa dear," said Thomas, "if you weren't a
woman I'd tell you in no uncertain terms to shut your
beautiful goddamned mouth. What's this got to do with
you anyway? You're not even involved! Why don't you
stop posing as the lady with the scales of justice and get
the hell out of our lives? I don't often agree with Neville, God knows, but this time I'm with him one
hundred percent. There's no point in going to the police. It's possible I might feel a little differently if April

were worth avenging, but I'm her brother and I'm prepared to let things be. We can achieve nothing by going to the police except a lot of grief for ourselves. Besides, it's all very well, Neville, for you to doubt whether the police could ever make an arrest, but supposing they did and arrested the wrong person."

"This is England," said Leonie. "Our police don't make mistakes like that."

"I bet they do," said Thomas. "They're only human, aren't they? Now supposing the police arrested Karen. She must be suspect number one as far as motive goes, but not even her worst enemy (you perhaps, Melissa dear?) could ever believe her guilty of murder."

"Just a moment, Thomas," interposed Neville. "Let's not start speculating about guilt and motive. Let's just concentrate on whether we're going to tell the police about the clothes. I personally am against it. So are you, Thomas. Karen darling—"

"I'm against it too," Karen heard herself say, and thought instinctively of the police questioning Neville, suspecting him, putting him under arrest . . .

"So am I," said Leonie at once with a fervor that Karen found surprising. She must have realized the extent of her brother's danger. "There's nothing to be gained from going to the police now. She was a most unpleasant girl—although I suppose I shouldn't say that—and she's dead and that's all there is to it. It would be senseless to resurrect it all now."

"Well, well, well," said Melissa. "What a united front all of a sudden!"

Nobody spoke. Then: "I still think Marney should know about this," said Leonie stubbornly. "Let me phone him, Neville."

"If we're not going to the police I see no point in worrying him with it."

"But I think he has a right to know," Leonie persisted. "He was, after all, involved—he was here three years ago, and even though he was staying at the lodge, he knew his way around the farm and this side of the valley. He's one of the five whom the police would suspect."

"But we're not going to the police."

"May I," said Melissa, "just ask one question? What makes you so sure that the child won't talk? He's given the game away once—how can you be so certain he won't do it again?"

"He doesn't know the significance the clothes have," said Neville. "As far as he's concerned the buried treasure turned out to be a big disappointment. He'll soon forget about it."

"You're crazy," said Melissa frankly. "All of you— you're quite mad. The whole thing's bound to come out and you'll all be charged—not with murder, perhaps but with conspiracy to conceal a murder—"

"I hope," said Thomas, "that you're not proposing to interfere in any way, Melissa."

"Well, if you think I'm going to sit back and implicate myself in all this, you couldn't be more wrong! I for one don't intend to be charged with conspiracy!" She ground her cigarette to ashes and stood up. "If someone hasn't informed the police before noon tomorrow, I most certainly shall."

There was a silence. She looked up suddenly, as if she found the silence surprising and saw everyone's eyes watching her.

"Melissa," said Thomas politely, "this is none of your—business."

"It most certainly is if you involve me in your conspiracy!" Melissa retorted. She moved to the door. "Well, I'm going. Perhaps someone could row me across to Kildoun."

There was another pause. Then:

"I will," said Neville.

"Thank you," said Melissa very pointedly, "but no. I'm sure someone else would do just as well. Perhaps you would, Thomas."

"Not on your sweet-natured little life! Row yourself."

The silence was so intense that it became almost audible.

"I'll row you across," said Leonie at last. "I'm used to the journey." Her tone of voice implied that she had reached the stage where she would welcome any opportunity to take Melissa as far away as possible. "But first I'm going to phone Marney and tell him what's happened."

"No, don't tell him a word on the phone," Neville ordered abruptly. "The local telephone operator might overhear something. Just ask Marney to drive over for dinner."

"Dinner! My God, I'd forgotten it! Everything will be terribly overdone." She hurried off anxiously towards the kitchen.

"I wish you'd let me row you over, Melissa," said Neville irritated. "Leonie's got more than enough to do here at the moment. What do you expect me to do— push you in the lake in broad daylight?"

"It's clouding over and getting very dark, as a matter of fact."

"Oh, for God's sake!"

"I'll wait till Leonie's ready, thank you."

"Thomas—" began Neville.

"No," said Thomas. "Absolutely not. *You* might not be tempted to push her into the lake but I most certainly would."

"Thomas!" Karen protested. "Don't, don't make such a joke just now . . ."

Neville was beside her in an instant. "Darling, why don't you lie down upstairs for a few minutes? You look exhausted and I'm not surprised. I'll bring your supper up to you in bed."

"I'm not hungry." She turned aside, conscious of a longing to escape. "But I think I will lie down."

Neville kissed her, and she made her way upstairs as quickly as possible. To her amazement she noticed that her legs were weak and her hands were trembling. When she reached her room she lay down on the bed for several moments, her eyes closed, her mind numb, and then directly below her in the dining-room she heard Leonie ask the operator for the number of the lodge at Plantation Q.

The telephone was by the window in the dining-room, and the window, like the window in the bedroom, was obviously wide open. Karen heard Leonie's voice travel clearly towards her on the still evening air.

"Dr. West, please . . . Marney? Could you come over to dinner? Something quite awful's happened, and —would you? Thank God . . . Yes, come as soon as you can."

There was a faint noise as the receiver was replaced.

Presently Neville said from somewhere at hand: "Is he coming?"

"Yes, he's coming straight away. Now, let me get rid of that dreadful woman."

There were footsteps, the murmur of distant voices, and then at last silence. Karen struggled to keep awake and think clearly about the situation confronting them all, but her nervous exhaustion coupled with the physical exercise of the walk to the lodge earlier made sleep impossible to combat. Almost without realizing it she had slipped into unconsciousness, and when she next opened her eyes she heard the roar of the jeep as Marney arrived at last from Plantation Q.

3

She rose, changed into a dress, adjusted her hair. When she was ready she went next door to Snuff's room to suggest it was time he went to bed, but Leonie had evidently been there before her for Snuff himself was sitting up in bed in his pajamas with his favorite well-worn story-book open before him. He seemed flattered that she had called in to say goodnight, and she stayed with him for a few minutes to read aloud to him from the book. Finally when she could put off the moment no longer she went downstairs and through the dining-room to the living-room where Neville was handing Marney a double whisky and soda. Thomas was propping up the window frame, an alert expression in his eyes, but there was no sign of Leonie; evidently she had not yet returned from rowing Melissa across to Kildoun. Karen glanced out of the window to see if she could see the boat, but outside heavy clouds had brought an early twilight and inside the light from the lamps made the windowpane a mirror reflecting the interior of the room.

Everyone turned to look at her.

"Good evening, Karen," said Marney, rising to his feet in an automatic gesture of courtesy. He looked tired, she noticed, and there was a strained set to his mouth. "Neville's just told me what's been happening here today."

She did not know what to say. She heard herself murmur awkwardly: "We thought you should know."

There was a pause. Then: "Well, there you have it," said Thomas abruptly. "Either we go to the police before noon tomorrow or else Melissa does the job for us. It's as simple as that."

Marney sat down again, sipped his drink and clasped the glass tightly in his long bony fingers. "Then it looks as if one way or the other the police will be informed, doesn't it?"

The comment drew no response.

"It's a pity someone can't persuade Melissa . . ." Marney let the sentence trail off into vagueness.

"Her mind's made up," said Neville flatly. "Besides, she's enjoying her position of power over me. There's nothing more I could say which would dissuade her."

Marney turned to Thomas. "Since you arrived with her, I assume you've both been seeing a lot of each other. Isn't it possible that you would be able to persuade her—"

"She's not my mistress, if that's what you mean," said Thomas righteously at once.

"That wasn't what I meant," said Marney without

inflection. "It just occurred to me that if you were at all friendly with her—"

"I'm not."

Marney shrugged. "Well,. there's certainly nothing I can do," he said at last. "There's no reason on earth why she should listen to me."

The front door opened. The next moment Leonie was moving into the room.

"Marney, thank God you're here—"

Karen was surprised how distraught Leonie looked. Her face was haggard, her hair straggling, her movements staccato with her nervousness.

"Has Neville told you? Neville, what have you said? Did you tell him—"

"Yes, yes," said Neville, poorly concealing his irritation at this display of panic. "We've just been talking about it. Sit down, Leonie, for God's sake, and relax and let me get you a drink. It won't solve anything if you get worked up over all this."

"Have my chair," said Marney at once, and insisted in installing her in it while she smiled up at him gratefully.

"So kind . . . thank you . . . perhaps we really ought to eat dinner straight away—if we wait much longer it'll be ruined—"

"Never mind about the dinner for the moment," said Neville dryly. "That's the least of our worries. The question is what are we going to do about Melissa?"

"A curiously sinister word-choice, Neville," Marney was smiling slightly. "What on earth can we 'do' with Melissa? Come, let's be realistic about this. There's nothing we can do. We can't persuade her to change her mind, and obviously if we attempt to force her

hand in any way it will only underline our own guilty
feelings."

"But Marney," said Leonie white-lipped, "Marney—"

"Look Marney," said Thomas. "You may not be directly involved in this, but we are—"

"Actually that's incorrect, Thomas. I'm every bit as
involved as you are. I know the farm and this side of
the mountain almost as well as I know Plantation Q,
and I knew April was staying here three years ago. If
the police investigate this I shall come under suspicion,
just as you will."

"Well, then—"

"Listen," said Marney, leaning forward in his chair,
"if we try to bargain with Melissa we make it look as if
we have something to hide—as if one of us really did
kill April three years ago." He paused. "One of us, you
understand? You, Neville—or Karen—or Thomas—or
you, Leonie—or myself. Now, let me ask you all this:
are we sure that one of us is guilty? How can we be?"

"You're surely not expecting a confession, Marney,"
said Thomas ironically.

"No," said Marney, "I'm not. Because I don't believe any one of us is guilty of murder. How do we
know April was murdered? We don't. There's no body.
All we have is pure conjecture. Supposing she had an
accident, for example—supposing she was accidentally
killed in such a way that to any outsider it might seem
that she had been murdered? That would account for
the fact that someone very much concerned buried the
clothes and created an impression that she had left. Or
else supposing, again, that she had an accident, and
someone seized on the opportunity to spare another

person all the distress of an inquest and inquiry by deliberately creating the impression that April was still alive while he himself removed all trace of her from the scene of the accident? Or supposing April herself packed her bags, took them to the jetty and then slipped, hit her head and drowned in a few feet of water nearby? Whoever buried the suitcases wouldn't even have had to go into the house to pack her clothes. You see how insubstantial all your theory of murder is? There's no evidence of murder, none at all. Certainly the police could never prove a murder charge against any one of us—they would suspect, yes, but suspicion and proof are two very different things. Even if they find the body, and it's just possible, I suppose, that they might, they'd still have no proof of who killed her. If she was killed at all. I don't think we have anything to fear from the police. If Melissa didn't intend to go to them with the whole story, I'd let the matter rest, but since she's made up her mind to tell them about the clothes I think we should be first to contact them. We should show them that we've nothing to hide."

"But Marney," said Leonie, "the investigations, the publicity, the police searching for the body—"

"If they find the body and find April's skull smashed in," said Thomas, "they won't think it's an accident, Marney."

"How do you know April's skull's smashed in?"

"The point is," said Thomas, "how do you know it isn't? Personally if I were a policeman, I'd be a lot more inclined to believe the murder theory than the accident theory, and I'd guess that it'd be a hell of a lot easier to prove murder than accident."

"I don't think the police would ever be able to prove anything."

"I think they could," said Neville unexpectedly. "They could establish motive and opportunity in some cases."

"That's still not proof, Neville."

"Hell," said Thomas. "Do your police expect every case to have the proof neatly displayed on a silver platter? I'll bet they don't! I'll bet they're as eager to make two and two make four as any other police force, and just as eager to accept circumstantial evidence."

"I think we're losing track of the argument," said Marney. "The point is that Melissa's going to the police. If we contact them before she does we create a good impression. If we leave her to tell the story we all look guilty. The police are going to ask us all why we didn't contact them as soon as we discovered the suitcases, why we haven't in fact contacted them at all. Can't you see how it's going to look to them?"

"I suppose," Karen said slowly, "we couldn't destroy the clothes—and the suitcases?"

Everyone stared at her.

"I mean, if we took them away and the police came and found nothing . . . We could easily make Melissa out to have been motivated by jealousy into making a false accusation—"

"That's a marvelous idea!" cried Leonie, flushing in her relief and enthusiasm. "Why didn't we think of that before?"

"Of course!" said Thomas, snapping his fingers. "You're a smart girl, Karen. That'll take care of Melissa and make her look like a fool, and it'll save us all the public resurrection of the past."

"We could burn the clothes," Neville mused, "and scatter the remains in the lake."

Leonie sprang to her feet. "Let's do it now."

"No!" said Marney so strongly that she jumped. He set down his glass. "I'm afraid I can't possibly agree to that—I'm surprised you agree to it, Neville. It may make Melissa look a fool, but the police are going to say 'no smoke without a fire' and make inquiries just the same. Besides, you're all entirely forgetting Snuff. If the police question him he'll tell them all about the clothes—how can he do otherwise? How can we ask a child of seven to lie to the police for reasons beyond his comprehension?"

Oh God, thought Karen stricken. She had forgotten. So deep was her confusion and anxiety that she had even forgotten that it was Snuff who had discovered the clothes.

"I suppose that argument's unanswerable," said Neville with reluctance, and even Thomas and Leonie had no defence to make.

There was a heavy silence.

"Let's have dinner," said Neville abruptly. "Maybe my brain will function better after I've had something to eat."

Dinner was a sombre meal. Afterwards over coffee they tried to discuss the situation again, but the arguments became circular and it became evident that no decision was likely to be reached. Marney maintained that they should go to the police at once, but no one was prepared to accept this as a tolerable solution to Melissa's ultimatum. In the end Thomas stood up and moved to the door.

"Look," he said, "let me row myself back to Kildoun

and spend the night in my room there. I'll have a talk with Melissa and exert a little charm and see if I can't persuade her to change her mind. Would you agree to wait till tomorrow morning, Marney?"

Marney shrugged. "The longer we leave it the worse it'll look to the police, but if everyone agrees to wait till tomorrow morning then I suppose I'm prepared to wait too."

"I'll call you first thing tomorrow, Neville," Thomas said, "and let you know if I had any success."

After he had gone they all remained in the living-room and discussed the situation further. Leonie was very over-wrought still, Karen noticed, and was constantly getting up and moving restlessly over to the window and then back to the chair again. Marney was drinking steadily, the glass of whiskey never leaving his hand except to be refilled. Neville was chain-smoking, and so was she, cigarette for cigarette, almost inhalation for inhalation, her nerves seemed unable to get enough of the soothing benefits of the drug.

Suddenly the phone rang. Neville leapt to his feet and picked up the receiver. "Hello? Yes, Thomas. What—you didn't? . . . Why? . . . I see . . . yes, all right, I'll tell them . . . Thanks." He replaced the receiver and slowly turned to face them.

"What's happened?" said Leonie tautly.

"Melissa wouldn't answer when he knocked on her door. She wouldn't even answer when he rang through to her room on the telephone. I'm afraid it seems she's quite determined not to reach a compromise."

Seven

1

When Neville had finished speaking there was a silence. At last Karen heard herself say slowly: "What are we going to do now?"

"Nothing." Neville began to mix himself another drink. "Thomas said he'd try to talk to Melissa in the morning and that he'd phone back again after breakfast."

"So we wait until tomorrow?"

"I don't see what else we can do."

There was another uneasy silence. Then: "That stupid interfering woman!" Leonie burst out, and Karen saw with a shock that her mouth was trembling and her eyes were bright with tears. "Why does she want to create trouble for us all? Why did she even have to come here?"

Marney stood up as if he suddenly wanted to escape. "I think I must be going back to the lodge, Neville. It's getting late, and it doesn't seem as if there's anything more we can do at the moment. Thank you for the dinner, Leonie."

Leonie made an effort to compose herself. "I'll come and see you off."

"No—no, please don't trouble—"

"Don't forget your coat. It's hanging up on the back door." She went out of the room to get it for him, and he wandered out after her, his head bowed, his shoulders hunched as if to ward off the memory of Melissa's ultimatum. "Good night, Karen. I'll see you tomorrow, Neville."

"All right, Marney. Goodnight."

He left. A minute later they heard the roar of his jeep as the engine flared into life, and then the noise receded as the jeep crawled away up the mountain track.

"I think—" Karen began, but was interrupted as Leonie called out from the kitchen: "Oh, he's left some papers behind! They must have fallen out of his coat pocket in the dark and he didn't notice."

"Never mind," said Neville. "I'll take them over to the lodge with me tomorrow."

"All right. Well, no, perhaps I'll go after him now. If I take your jeep he'll see the headlights behind him and wait for me to catch him up so I won't have to drive all the way over to the lodge. Anyway I want to get away from the farm for a little while. I feel one of my headaches coming on and I'm sure I'll never be able to sleep if I try to go to bed now. Do you have the keys to the jeep, Neville?"

"They're in the ignition."

"I feel the opposite to Leonie," said Karen to Neville as the back door closed and they were alone together. "I'm exhausted and all I want to do is to fall into bed and sleep for twelve hours." She did not add that she wanted to escape from further discussion of Melissa. "What are you going to do now, darling?"

"I may join you soon." He was by the window, his hands in his pockets, and he did not turn to face her as he spoke. "I think I'll go for a short walk. I feel very restless and the exercise will probably calm me down."

"I'll see you later, then," said Karen and went upstairs without further delay. When she reached the room she closed the door and then moved over to the window to stare outside for a long moment. All trace of that gloomy clouded twilight had now faded into suffocating darkness; night had come, and suddenly dawn seemed intolerably distant, as if it lay at the far end of an interminable corridor of time.

Karen undressed slowly and spent a long time preparing herself for bed. It was as if she had changed her mind and were putting off the moment of inactivity as long as possible, clinging to any mundane movement which would help take her mind off the situation. Everywhere was very quiet. She wondered vaguely if Leonie had managed to catch up with Marney before he reached the pass.

At length the time came when there was nothing else to do but pull back the covers and slip between the sheets. She turned down the lamp, but presently the darkness seemed too overpowering so she slipped out of bed and drew back the curtains.

To her surprise she found the heavy clouds had broken and were drifting stormily across the face of a ragged moon. The scene had the eerie silver-black quality of an unreal landscape delineated in some strange medium. Karen shivered, turned aside, but could not bring herself to go back to bed. Presently she went downstairs. There was no one there, but the lamp was still burning in the living-room and the ashes still flickered in the grate from the evening fire. Karen had a sudden absurd wave of revulsion against being alone in the house. Shaking herself resolutely she walked to the decanter, mixed herself a stiff scotch and soda, and with the glass in her hands sat down on the couch and gazed at the red embers in the grate. But the blankness of the dark windows forced themselves to her attention; seconds later she was standing up to draw the curtains.

It was very quiet.

Of course she was not alone in the house. Snuff was there too, upstairs, fast asleep. Lucky Snuff, able to dismiss the suitcases as mere disappointing buried treasure.

She began to move restlessly about the room, but presently even the shuffle of her slippers sounded so loud that she stopped to listen. The silence closed in on her at once, stifling walls of soundlessness. She began to walk up and down again.

It was foolish to be nervous, she told herself, foolish and neurotic. If the farm were by the road on the other side of the lake she would have had an excuse to be nervous of the loneliness, but here the very isolation made it perfectly safe. There was no chance of a visit from some stray hitchhiker, not even the threat of a passing car.

She opened the door, moved through the dining-room and paused by the front door. It was unlocked. Neville always left it unlocked while they were staying at the house. There was no reason to lock it because there was no possibility of intrusion. It was so safe, so isolated.

Karen stared at the door. Supposing it were to open now. She pictured it swinging silently inwards on its hinges, motivated by some hidden force outside, and there on the threshold was April, her body rotted from three years in the black soft earth, her eyes bright and insanely alive.

Karen leant back against the wall and closed her eyes. She must not, would not give way to hysteria. She forced herself to look at the closed door calmly, and as she looked, willing herself to remain calm and self-possessed, she saw the door handle begin to turn slowly as if it had a life of its own.

"Neville!" The cry was a reflex born of panic, and then suddenly he was there beside her and closing the door behind him as he entered the hall.

"What's the matter, darling? You look white as a ghost! I'm sorry I was so long—I went further up the stream than I intended. Couldn't you sleep?"

"No, I guess I was more restless than I thought I was. Wasn't there any sign of Leonie returning?"

"None, but I doubt if she managed to catch Marney this side of the pass. Besides, she might have driven all the way to the lodge to have a private conference with him—that would be typical! I hope Marney doesn't have too much difficulty in getting rid of her if she turns up at the lodge." He moved towards the living-room. "I'm going to have one final drink and then I'll join you upstairs. I shan't be long."

She went back to their bedroom, her knees weak, her body trembling, and this time the effects of shock combined with the whisky so that she was glad to lie still and close her eyes.

She never even heard Neville come to bed.

When she awoke it was dark and someone was moving about the room.

"Neville?" she said nervously, still not fully awake.

"Yes, I can't sleep. I'm going downstairs for a while. Don't you worry—just go back to sleep and relax."

His voice was reassuring; unconsciousness was close at hand and presently she was slipping back into sleep again, her mind disturbed by brief flickers of dreams which made no sense and which memory would not retain. She was aware of tossing and turning but when she next opened her eyes it was dawn and the room was filled with a pale unearthly light.

Something was wrong. She twisted round in bed instinctively and then she recognized the source of her uneasiness. She was alone; Neville had never returned.

2

She went downstairs, but there was no sign of him. Still wearing only her nightdress and peignoir, she opened the back door and walked a few yards up the hillside behind the house so that she had an uninterrupted view of the surrounding country, but as far as the eye could see there was no hint of life. Neville's jeep was parked near the stream to indicate that Leoni had returned safely during the night, and the jeep seemed as small as a toy against the vastness of the mountains and the moors. The dawn was breathtaking in its translucent colors, but the air was cold; Karen shivered, drew her peignoir closer around her and returned to the house, but even after pausing in the kitchen, the warmest room in the house, she was still shivering. At length she was about to return to her room when she heard the noise of a door opening somewhere above her and the next moment Leonie, wearing a long drab dressing-gown, was coming quietly downstairs.

Leonie saw her and gave a start of surprise. "I thought I heard someone moving about! What's the matter? Couldn't you sleep?"

"Neville seems to have disappeared," Karen heard herself say, aware that Leonie was no longer a source of irritation but a welcome presence in the isolated silence. "I woke up in the middle of the night and found him about to go out for a walk as he couldn't sleep, but when I woke up again just now he still wasn't back."

"Did you notice the time when Neville left?"

"No—no, I didn't."

"It might only have been a short time ago—dawn has only just come and half an hour ago it was still dark." She crossed to the gas stove, reached for the kettle and filled it with water. "I couldn't sleep either. I'm going to have a cup of tea, but I suppose you'd rather have coffee."

"Please." They waited in silence while the water was heated, and presently they were sitting down together at the kitchen table with the steaming cups and Karen was watching the lake change color as the sun rose higher in the sky.

"I wish Neville would come back," she couldn't help saying. "I wonder where he can be."

"Perhaps he's gone over to the hotel to try to talk to Melissa," Leonie said unexpectedly. "I know Neville felt very strongly how important it was for Melissa to see reason about going to the police."

"But if Melissa won't change her mind, what could Neville do? We're all powerless."

"If anyone can persuade her," said Leonie firmly, "Neville will. He knows how important it is for all our sakes."

Karen was aware of irritation. "All?" she said. "But you won't be much affected if Melissa goes to the police! You were at the lodge when April disappeared—you weren't even here! You don't have to worry."

"Well, of course," said Leonie, bridling at Karen's tone of voice, "I don't worry on *my own* account. I'm worried about Neville—and you, naturally. And Marney."

Karen opened her mouth to say that Marney had been working on the plantation all morning on the day of April's disappearance, but then shut it again instinctively. Instead she said: "Yes, I guess the situation is awkward for Marney."

Leonie shot her a suspicious glance and took a sip of tea thoughtfully.

Karen changed her tactics. "Marney didn't see April that morning, did he?" she demanded, deciding on a direct approach. "He didn't come to the farm?"

There was a silence. "Well, actually," said Leonie after a long pause, "yes, he did."

"But I thought—" said Karen and stopped.

There was another long silence.

"Well, after all," said Leonie practically, "I might just as well tell you—we're all in the same boat. I'd already decided to tell Neville as soon as I had the opportunity, so I suppose it won't do any harm to tell you. Anyway perhaps you really should know the exact situation—especially now that we're all in such a dangerous position."

She absent-mindedly helped herself to more tea. The dark water swirled in the cup and a monstrous tea-leaf, swollen and bloated, floated to the surface and stayed there. Karen watched it drift around and around in circles as Leonie stirred the tea twice with her spoon.

"I left the farm at nine that morning," Leonie said at last. "The morning April disappeared, I mean. I got up early and had breakfast on my own. Neither April nor Neville were up, much to my relief, and I didn't see them before I left. I had arranged by phone the night before to meet Marney at the lodge at ten o'clock that day because I wanted his advice on how I should handle the situation—I was really so angry with Neville that I hardly trusted myself to speak to him at all, and I thought Marney could help me, tell me what to do."

The whirling eddies died in the tea-cup. She scooped out the monstrous tea-leaf with her spoon and laid it neatly in the saucer.

"After all," she was saying, "the farm *was* mine! Wouldn't you have felt angry if you'd been in my shoes? I know Neville insisted that April had chased after him without his consent, but . . . well, he wasn't exactly displeased to see her, you know! In my opinion he should have told her to stay at the hotel when she rang up from Kildoun to ask him to row across the lake to fetch her—but no! Such a thought obviously didn't enter his head. He brought her across to the farm as if they expected *me* to go to the hotel and leave them alone together! Really it was shameful how little consideration they had for my feelings! The whole episode was so degrading, so sordid." She shuddered suddenly at the memory. "So I decided to go over and see Marney. It took me about fifty minutes to walk over to the lodge, so by the time I arrived it was about ten minutes to ten. I was a bit early so I wasn't surprised when Marney wasn't there to meet me. I waited for a while in his office, and then one of the foresters came in and told me that Marney had gone out to the furthest boundary of the plantation to complete a project and wouldn't be back till lunch-time. He had forgotten all about my appointment with him—Marney's so absent-minded sometimes. Anyway I left him a note telling him what had happened and saying I wanted to see him, and then I walked back over the mountain to the farm.

"It was about eleven by the time I arrived, and the first thing I saw was the jeep parked by the stream. I was puzzled because Neville—and later April—had arrived by boat the night before, but I supposed that Neville had followed me over to the plantation, taken a jeep from the barn and driven back here while I had been in the lodge waiting for Marney. So I walked past it over the footbridge and slipped in the back door.

"I heard them almost at once. They were in the living-room. I went through the kitchen, across the hall and into the dining-room. The living-room door was ajar and I—well, I listened. I was too stupefied to do anything else, because it wasn't Neville with April at all. It was Marney. Marney had driven over to see April when everyone else thought he was out at work on the plantation. There was no sign of Neville, of course, although I didn't find out till later that he was searching for you on Plantation Q. I didn't even know of your arrival then because I had left the farm before Thomas had rowed you across the lake from the hotel at Kildoun.

"All I knew was that Marney and April were talking together in the living-room just a few feet away from me, and as I listened to the conversation I realized—" She stopped. An ugly red stain spread upwards from her neck. She was staring down into her tea, her elbows on the table, her hands clasped tightly together. At last she managed to add: "I realized they knew each other very well, much better than I'd ever imagined."

Karen was aware of shock. It took her a moment to speak. "You don't mean—you can't mean that April and Marney—"

Leonie said nothing.

"They couldn't have been having an affair! I don't believe it!"

"No," said Leonie, still not looking at her, "they weren't. But that was apparently what Marney wanted."

"My God . . ." Karen was too amazed to say more. She had been aware that Marney had admired April, but not that he had been infatuated with her.

"April seemed to find the idea quite amusing," said Leonie.

April would. Karen had a shaft of understanding. Marney wouldn't have been the first ascetic, self-contained man who had suddenly and for no obvious reason become blindly infatuated with a woman as unsuitable as April. No wonder April had been amused! Another man to her credit—another notch on the tallystick, but this time the man would have had no attraction for her whatever.

"I didn't stay after that," said Leonie in a muffled voice. "I was too shocked. I ran outside again, over the footbridge and along the lakeside past the ruined house. I walked and walked. I walked to the very tip of the lake, and after that I walked back again. I felt more composed by that time, more in control of myself, and physically I was too exhausted by all the exercise I had taken that morning even to summon the strength to make a disastrous scene. But I needn't have worried about making a scene. When I got back to the house at last, they had both gone and the place was deserted. After a while I began to wonder where Neville was so I telephoned the lodge and spoke to him there. He told me what had happened, said you had left with Thomas and he didn't know what to do. Then he said Marney had just come in from the plantation for lunch and he wanted to talk the situation over with him. In the end they both arrived at the house shortly afterwards, and it wasn't until then that we discovered April had packed, rowed herself across the lake and departed—or so we thought at the time. We were all so relieved. Later that day Neville and Marney left Scotland together, but I stayed on alone for another week to complete my holiday before rejoining Neville in London. I didn't know what to say to Marney about the scene I had overheard, so in the end I said nothing and never revealed that I knew he hadn't spent the whole morning at the plantation. I half-wondered if he would guess I'd seen him when he heard I'd been back at the farm by eleven, but Marney's so vague about time and while he was with April I'm sure he didn't stop to look at his watch. After leaving the house he must have driven straight to the section where he was supposed to be working; since he didn't go all the way back to the lodge he wouldn't have wondered later why he hadn't met me while I was walking back again over the mountain. He would simply have assumed later that he must have just missed seeing me before he turned off the main track to drive out to the remote section of the plantation where his work lay, and I thought it best not to let him know I had already reached the house before he left. I was right, wasn't I? It wouldn't have helped if I'd told him what I knew."

"Did you tell him when you saw him last night?"

"No, I didn't see him last night. I dropped the papers at the lodge and didn't stop to talk to him. Besides, I think he had gone straight up to bed."

"And you never told Neville?"

"Neville? Of course not! This was strictly between Marney and myself. Why should I have told Neville?"

"But if Marney was the last person to see April alive—"

"At the time we didn't think she was dead. We thought she had simply gone away."

"But now—"

"Oh, *now*," said Leonie impatiently. "Yes, I told you I was going to tell Neville about it as soon as I had the opportunity, but of course it still doesn't prove Marney had anything to do with April's death. Anyone could have gone to the house and killed her when Marney left in his jeep. I'm quite convinced that Marney left in his jeep. I'm quite convinced that Marney didn't kill her and that he's completely innocent of any crime."

Karen was silent. All she could think of was that

April had been seen and heard by two people after Neville had left her. Neville couldn't have killed her. Neville wasn't guilty.

"Don't you agree?" Leonie was persisting. "Someone could have killed her after Marney left. Don't you agree?"

"Yes," said Karen, anxious not to upset Leonie by disagreeing. "I guess so."

"Marney's innocent," repeated Leonie, her voice high and strained in that still room, and Karen suddenly began to wonder if Leonie was protesting Marney's innocence so loudly because she had seen him commit murder and wanted desperately to protect him.

3

The coffee tasted hot and bitter. Karen put down her cup after one sip, and stood up slowly. "Maybe I'll just slip outside again," she heard herself say, "to see if there's still no sign of Neville."

Leonie turned her head sharply. "But you do see, don't you, how important it is that Melissa shouldn't interfere in such a dangerous situation? You see how important it is that the police shouldn't be told?"

"Certainly I do, and I appreciate you telling me all this—it gives me a much clearer understanding of the situation." She escaped quickly, closing the back door behind her and taking deep lungfuls of the cool Highland air as she moved up the hillside again to the same vantage point.

There was still no sign of Neville. She wondered desperately where he could be and what had happened to him, and then decided that before she considered the problem further she should put on some thicker clothes to combat the chill of the northern morning. Ten minutes later, wearing warm slacks, a sweater and walking shoes she slipped out of the back door again and walked back to her vantage point to think clearly.

Perhaps Neville had walked over to Plantation Q to discuss the situation further with Marney. Yet would Neville have bothered to walk? Surely he would have taken his jeep and driven over to the lodge. Karen glanced back at the jeep parked near the stream and decided that in all probability Neville had not gone to Plantation Q. Yet despite Leonie's suggestion, Karen doubted if Neville would have gone to see Melissa at dawn when the hotel doors would be locked and Melissa would certainly be asleep. So where could Neville be?

She paced about restlessly, aware of her extreme tension and the gnawing ache of anxiety. Perhaps after all Neville had walked over the mountain—he himself had said earlier that he felt exercise would calm him down, so perhaps on this one occasion he had walked instead of using the jeep.

He must have walked. He would be at the lodge and talking to Marney.

"I'll walk over myself," she decided suddenly, and at once felt better for reaching a decision. She felt herself unable to endure waiting any longer, and she had an immense desire to escape from Leonie and talk to Neville of the new suspicions which had insinuated their way into her mind and now refused to be put aside.

"I must find Neville," she thought, "I have to find Neville. I must talk to him."

She walked back to the farm, crossed the stream and went on past the parked jeep up the mountain track. Once or twice she glanced back at the farm, but Leonie evidently had not seen her, or if she had she was making no attempt at pursuit. Karen relaxed a little and began to walk at a more even pace so that the steep gradient would not exhaust her too soon, but presently her breathlessness drew her to a halt and she stood for a moment and looked back once more at the house now far below her on the floor of the valley.

The golden pallor of dawn had faded into the clear brightness of daylight; the sky was already streaked with clouds and across the valley to the west the mountains were partially obscured by mist. The moors were a curious shade of purple-brown, shifting and varying in hue as the clouds began to drift across the sun. Below, the lake was a long slender strip of immobility, sometimes blue as azure, sometimes dark as flint in the changing light. As far as the eye could see was nothing but magnificent yet oppressive isolation.

Karen reached the top of the pass and paused to get her breath, but in less than a minute she was moving on again. She was beginning to feel more urgently than ever that she must talk to Neville, warn him about Marney. What would Neville do? What would he say to Marney? There was so little time; Melissa would be going to the police at noon.

She was almost running now. The path was winding downhill, and directly ahead of her were the dark silent trees of the plantation, a direct contrast to the bare sweep of the surrounding moors. In a quarter of an hour—ten minutes—she could be at the lodge talking to Neville.

She stumbled on down the track, her eyes watching the ground to avoid the danger of tripping over a loose rock or stone. Soon she had reached the edge of the plantation and she slackened her pace again and glanced around her nervously. She had always hated the twilight of the woods, the unnatural stillness that prevailed there.

She saw the tire-tracks straight away. They bit into the wet earth and curved away around the perimeter of the plantation. They looked fresh and clear and clean-cut in the morning light, a trail blazed in darkness and now coming into its own as the sun rose steadily in the east.

Karen felt her heart bumping rapidly. She stopped, pushed the hair back from her forehead, and stared through the trees. Perhaps Neville—no, Neville wouldn't be working at this hour. Perhaps one of the foresters had just driven up from the lodge. Perhaps he would know if Neville was there talking to Marney.

She moved forward away from the path and followed the tire-marks skirting the edge of the woods. There was no sign of a jeep although Karen expected to see one with every step she took. She walked on, her feet making no noise on the soft pine-needles, her breath sounding hard and uneven in her throat, and suddenly it seemed to her in a flash of fantasy that all the trees were watching, waiting in anticipation as she drew nearer the end of the trail. Her scalp began to tingle, but she did not stop. Her feet carried her across the pine needles until abruptly the trail ended in a muddy swirl where the jeep had been turned around and driven back to the main track.

There seemed to be no one about.

She was aware of an immense fear. She cast a quick glance around her but there was nothing except the pines on one side of her and the open moors of the mountainside on the other. And then suddenly she saw the grave.

Her legs carried her forward against her will; it was as if she were drawn forward by compulsion.

There was a rectangular patch of freshly-dug black earth. A few pine needles had been scattered over it but there was no mistaking its sinister measurements. Karen picked up a stick, sank it into the soft earth and struck flesh.

After that she was hardly sure what happened. Hands which did not seem to belong to her scraped at the earth and revealed a wrist, a slim elegant wrist still looking repulsively human, and on the wrist beyond the costume ring Melissa always wore were Melissa's meticulously manicured fingernails, shining, polished, and horribly alive.

But Melissa was without doubt very dead.

Karen was dimly surprised that she did not feel dizzy, but when she stood up there was no roaring in her ears, no weakness in her legs. All she was aware of was the absolute stillness and the silent watching twilight of the woods.

She stared down again at the grave. She looked and went on looking in mesmerized disbelief, but at last she raised her eyes slowly to the dark silent shadows of the trees beyond the grave and it was then that she saw him, standing there.

Eight

1

Her hand went to her mouth. She took a pace backwards.

"Karen!" His eyes were wide and blank. "My God, what are you doing here?"

She tried to move, but could not. She tried to speak but the words would not come. And then he began to walk towards her and the fear rose in her throat and forced her to cry out loud.

"No, Marney—"

He did not stop. He came on towards her without hesitation, his footsteps soundless on the pine-needles, and suddenly, mercifully, the power to move returned to her and she was running blindly downhill through the dark trees, the harsh sobs jolting her body. He was running after her. She could hear him behind her but

such was her terror that she did not even look back.
How far was it down to the lodge? How long could she
keep running like this? Supposing she should get lost.
And she thought of that other time three years ago
when she had rushed out of the house to escape from
April and Neville and had lost herself hopelessly
among the acres of trees.

The questions stabbed through her thoughts and
seemed to cast jagged patterns across her consciousness.
She had reached the track again now after cutting a di-
agonal path through the woods, and as her feet slid
painfully against the rough stones she looked back for
the first time and saw Marney swerving deeper into the
woods.

Perhaps he was heading to cut her off. He knew the
plantation so much better than she did. Still sobbing
with her exhaustion and panic she ran into the woods
on the other side of the track and began to run downhill among the trees again. As long as she kept moving
downhill she knew she would eventually reach the level
of the lodge. And once she reached the lodge she would
be safe.

A minute later a crippling stitch made her stop and
bend over double. She was fighting for breath. Perhaps
she would never get to the lodge. Perhaps Marney
would catch up with her in a matter of seconds. She
twisted round, but he was nowhere in sight. Had he lost
her? Or was he hiding, watching her? Her thoughts
spun dizzily, but even before she could attempt to answer her own questions, the pain in her side eased and
she was running again.

The trees thinned; she came upon a wide cut through
the woods, and as she crossed it she saw him watching

her far over to the left. He would have known she had
to cross the cut to reach the lodges, and as she stumbled across the open track to the trees on the other side
she was aware with horror that he was now probably
between her and the lodge itself. She had struck a
course out to the west of the mountain track, and
wherever Marney placed himself between her and the
track he would succeed in cutting her off.

In panic she began to make a still wider detour,
moving even further out to the west. She must come
round in a circle and approach the lodge from the
front. There was no other way. If only she didn't get
lost she might still reach safety.

The trees closed in on her again and met above her
head to obscure the early morning sunlight. Karen
began to feel as if she were suffocating in some terrible
grave. She had stopped running now on account of exhaustion and was half-walking, half-stumbling down
the hillside slopes. And then at last she realized that the
ground was no longer tilted beneath her feet, and that
she was on a different terrain. The lodge would be to
her left now. Cautiously, her eyes straining to pierce
the gloom and detect any possible sign of a pursuer,
she began to move to the left.

Ten minutes later she stumbled on the drive which
linked the lodge to the main road, and keeping among
the trees for protection she changed course again and
pressed northwards up to the lodge.

Suddenly she saw the barn ahead of her where the
fleet of jeeps was kept. The house lay beyond, its walls
mellow and tranquil in the morning light. Karen was
ready to collapse with sheer relief. The tears of reaction
were just pricking her eyelids when a car roared from

the drive behind her and the next moment a white Fiat
600 flashed past and swung off the road to cruise to a
halt on one side of the barn.

Karen had shrunk back instinctively into the trees as
the car had passed her, but now she ran forward, summoning up new reserves of strength which she did not
know she possessed. Rushing round the corner of the
barn, she bumped straight into the man who was
emerging from the driver's seat.

"Neville!" She was almost hysterical with relief. "Oh
Neville, Neville, Neville—"

He was just in time to catch her as she fainted.

2

When she next opened her eyes she found she was lying
on the sofa in Neville's study at the lodge. Neville was
sitting beside her holding one of her hands, and beyond
him was Thomas, his face white, his eyes bright with
anxiety.

"Thomas?" She groped dimly for some memory of
what had happened and then remembered that Thomas
had been in the passenger seat as Neville had emerged
from the little Fiat. "What happened?" she said confused. "I don't understand. Why are you both here?"

They glanced at each other quickly. "We came to
look for Marney," said Thomas. "But while you were
unconscious just now Neville checked his room and he
wasn't there."

"I rowed myself over to Kildoun as soon as dawn
came," explained Neville. "The more I thought about it
the less I understood why Melissa had failed to answer

when Thomas knocked on her door and rang her room last night. Before I left I telephoned the manager MacPherson and he very nobly rose to the occasion, got out of bed and let me into the hotel when I arrived. We then discovered Melissa wasn't in her room, although all her clothes were still there and her car was still parked in the yard. Then Thomas—"

"I woke up next door and wanted to know what was going on." Thomas shifted warily from one foot to the other. "Neville and I had a conference and decided to drive round by road in Melissa's car to the lodge to see if Marney knew anything about the mystery. Karen honey, I hate to rush you but can you tell us now what you were doing here? Do you feel strong enough yet to tell us what's happening?"

"I didn't know where Neville was . . ." She still felt muddled. "I thought you must have walked over to the lodge for some reason, Neville, so I—"

"Didn't you see that both boats were missing from the jetty? Thomas took one last night and I took the other this morning."

"No, I—how stupid of me! I never thought to check the jetty or the boathouse. I simply thought you couldn't have gone across to see Melissa while it was still so early."

"Did you have some urgent reason for wanting to see me?"

"Yes, I—oh God, yes, I did . . ." She began to talk. She heard her voice, a low even monotone recounting her conversation with Leonie, her conviction that Leonie suspected Marney of murder, her journey over the mountain, the grave, the confrontation with Marney, the chase . . . Suddenly she broke off and shuddered as the shock of memory began to exist in comprehensible terms.

"Get her some more brandy, Thomas. There's another bottle in that cupboard over there. Well, it all seems plain enough, doesn't it? Marney must have killed April three years ago and he must have killed Melissa last night. I've no doubt we'll find April's grave close to Melissa's in that same section of the plantation."

"I should think so. The situation was probably aggravated by the fact that she was involved with me."

"Yeah, that makes sense. That gives him a motive, and that's what floored us when we were trying to figure out the situation just now at the hotel. Do you think Leonie saw him kill her?"

"No, I don't. If she had seen him kill her, I'm sure she would have said something, if not to me then to Marney himself. Good God, she could even have forced him to marry her if she'd witnessed him commit murder! At least she would have promised him her loyalty and sworn herself to eternal secrecy. She wouldn't have been able to keep the information to herself for three years."

"Then you think—"

"I think she was telling Karen the truth. She overheard part of the quarrel, then dashed out to recover from the shock and waited until she was exhausted. By the time she returned to the house Marney had killed April and driven the body off in his jeep for burial on the edge of the plantation."

"But would he have had time to pack the suitcases and tow the spare boat across the lake?"

"Plenty of time. If Leonie walked to the tip of the lake she would have been gone for well over an hour. He was alone at the house—and what's more as far as he knew he was certain to be alone there; he didn't know, remember, that you and Karen had arrived and had stayed the night at Kildoun. He only knew I was staying at the house with April and Leonie, and since Leonie was by that time at the lodge waiting for him (or so he thought) and since he naturally assumed I was at the plantation beginning my business by the time he arrived at the house to see April, he couldn't have foreseen any interruption. It all fits in."

The brandy was beginning to make Karen feel better. She had stopped shivering and her brain was becoming clearer. She drank the last drop determinedly and set the empty glass down on the table with a steady hand. "But Neville," she said evenly, "how could Marney have killed Melissa? I don't understand."

"Easy," said Neville at once. "As soon as he got back to the lodge last night he must have taken Kelleher's Rolls and driven round by road to the hotel at Kildoun. Unless—Karen, did Leonie say she saw Marney last night when she drove after him with those papers?"

"No, she didn't see him. She said she thought he had probably gone to bed and she simply left the papers at the lodge."

"There you are, then! Marney left immediately, arrived at Kildoun and sought Melissa out to discuss the situation. When she refused to change her mind about going to the police he killed her, drove her back to the lodge and finally took the body up to the top of the plantation for burial."

"You mean he killed her at the hotel?" Karen said doubtfully.

"No, I expect he suggested a drive in his car to talk the situation over."

"But how did he get in touch with her when he reached the hotel? She refused to speak to Thomas."

"Maybe he simply knocked on her door and told her who he was. Melissa would have been intrigued to know what he wanted. She probably hadn't foreseen an interview with Marney."

"But how did he know which room she had?"

"Couldn't he simply have asked? He's known at the hotel and they wouldn't have seen anything odd about him wanting a word with one of the English guests who happened to be known to him."

"What do we do now?" said Thomas abruptly before Karen could say anything else. "Shall we call the police?"

"I'd like to see Marney first. Damn it, where is he? If he was running after Karen he should have been here ten minutes ago! Perhaps he realized he couldn't catch Karen and decided to go over to the house to see me and try to explain away what had happened. After all, he doesn't know I'm here. He thinks I'm asleep in bed. Perhaps we'd better drive back over the mountain to the house."

"Then he's sure to come back here and we'll miss him," said Thomas sardonically.

"All right," said Neville, making up his mind. "You stay here at the lodge, Thomas, in case he comes back, and I'll take Karen over to the farm with me. I'm not letting her out of my sight after her adventures this morning."

"What do I say to Marney if he turns up here?"

"Tell him to drive over to the house to see me. Say I know everything but I'd like a word with him before I actually telephone the police."

"Okay then." Thomas looked uneasy for a moment, but soon managed to suppress any trace of nervousness. "Is that all right with you, Karen? How are you feeling now?"

"I'm better, Thomas, don't worry about me." She stood up and was surprised to find herself light-headed after drinking brandy on an empty stomach. "I don't mind going back with Neville."

"I'd better take another jeep," murmured Neville, rising to his feet. "Kelleher will be cross since I've already got one at the house, but I can't help that. Are you ready to leave now, darling, or do you want to wait a few minutes longer?"

Karen said she was ready. She now felt so tense again that she longed for some kind of action. The more she waited the more nervous she became.

Neville brought one of the jeeps up to the door and helped her up into the passenger seat.

"I'll see you later, Thomas."

"Okay, Neville. Good luck. Take care, Karen."

"You too, Thomas. 'Bye."

The jeep was rattling off across the yard towards the main cut into the woods, and Thomas stood on the doorstep looking after them, a small lost figure shading his eyes against the sunlight.

There was no sign of Marney. At the perimeter of the plantation, Neville halted the jeep to examine the trail of tire-marks for himself and to look at the grave.

He came back three minutes later, his mouth grim and set, his hands clenched deep in his pockets.

"No sign of him," was all he said. "The place was deserted."

They did not speak again until they reached the farm, parked the jeep and crossed the bridge over the burn to the back door.

"I think he's here," muttered Neville. "I can hear Leonie talking to someone in the kitchen."

Karen felt the breath catch in her throat. Her nails dug into the palms of her hands.

Neville opened the back door.

The voices stopped. Then:

"So there you are, Neville," said Marney in a strange hard voice. "I'm glad you've come back because I was just about to telephone the police and I wanted a word with you before I spoke to them. You bloody fool! You might have got away with April's murder, but what on earth made you think you could get away with Melissa's? Why the devil did you have to lose your head and kill her?"

3

There was a long amazed silence. Neville had stopped abruptly and was for once at a loss for words. Leonie, looking drawn and haggard, had her back to the sink and Marney was standing by the stove. To Karen, on the threshold of the room, the scene seemed like a tableau hovering on the brink of some appalling animation.

"You did kill her, didn't you," said Marney, still

speaking in his strange hard voice. His hands were clenched in tension, his scanty hair was windblown and untidy, his clothes muddy and creased. As he spoke he kept pausing to lick his lips. "You weren't out on the plantation for three hours searching for Karen the day April was killed. You walked to the lodge to get a jeep and then you drove back to the house after I had left and Leonie was far away at the tip of the lake. You found April alone and after you had killed her you drove her body up to the plantation and buried it near the place where you buried Melissa last night. If Karen hadn't interrupted me this morning I'm certain I would have found April's grave just a few yards from Melissa's. I got up early because I couldn't sleep and decided to walk over to the house to have breakfast with all of you—but then I saw the tire-marks running off the track and around the edge of the trees, and since I couldn't understand why anyone should have been in that section of the plantation I went to see what had been going on. Then Karen came. I tried to catch her to ask her how much she knew but when I lost her I decided to continue my journey to the house to have it out with you once and for all. How did you kill Melissa? I suppose you rowed across the lake last night and suggested you go for a drive in her car while you discussed the situation. Then you must have killed her, taken her to the lodge and driven the body by jeep up to that section of the plantation. Am I right? After that you simply drove back to the lodge and returned Melissa's car to the hotel before rowing across the lake to the house again. That's what happened, isn't it? Wasn't that what you did?"

Neville found his voice at last. "You know damned

well I did no such thing," he said. He seemed mesmerized by Marney's transformation into an angry counsel for the prosecution. "You know bloody well you killed them both."

Leonie shook her head violently: "Don't—don't, Neville—"

Neville swung round to face her. "Leonie, it's too late for lies now. It's impossible to cover up for one another or pretend we can all overlook murder to save ourselves unpleasantness with the police. Melissa's dead—killed—buried up on the plantation with April—"

"So you admit it," said Marney. "You admit April's buried up on the plantation with Melissa." He moved towards the door leading into the hall. "I'm going to phone the police, tell them everything and suggest they look around for April's grave while they exhume Melissa."

Neville suddenly seemed to realize that Marney was in earnest. "You're going to tell the police that because you know damned well they'll find April there!" he shouted. "Your only hope of getting out of this unscathed is to try to blame everything on me!"

"Shout as much as you like," said Marney. "You won't convince me you're not guilty. Who else could have killed those two women? Leonie could never have buried April on the plantation because she could never have transported the body there from the house—she had no jeep. Karen couldn't conceivably have killed Melissa since she was at the house all last night. Thomas might have killed them both but he would never have buried the bodies in that particular place. He doesn't know the plantation well enough and he had no access to the jeeps anyway. So it's you or I, Neville, and since I know perfectly well that I could never— never, you understand—deprive another human being of life, that leaves you." He turned abruptly on his heel. "I'm going to call the police."

Karen heard herself call dizzily: "No, wait, Marney, wait—" But she was interrupted.

"But Marney," said Leonie in a loud harsh voice, "April's not buried on the plantation."

"Leonie my dear, I know you want to protect your brother, but I really feel that the time has come to tell the truth—"

"But I am telling the truth," said Leonie. Her eyes were dark and huge in their sockets; her mouth was working grotesquely. "I killed April and last night I killed Melissa. Don't you understand what I'm saying? I killed them. I killed them both."

4

They stared at her in silent disbelief, and as they stared she began to wring her hands, squeezing her long fingers until the bones cracked. "I killed April after you left, Marney. I waited till you had driven away in your jeep and then I slipped back into the house and killed her. I didn't mean to but I had had such a shock in discovering you were in love with her that I couldn't have been quite sane. I shook her so hard that she fell and stunned herself, and then when she was unconscious I gripped her throat until she didn't breathe any more."

"Leonie—" Neville, appalled, tried to argue with her, but she refused to listen to him.

"No, it's true, Neville, it's true! And I killed Melissa last night. I took her down to the water's edge to row her across the lake to the hotel and it was so dark, so gloomy with all those clouds hiding the mountains that I couldn't help thinking that no one would see me if . . . I didn't really stop to think, you see. I pretended I had to go into the boathouse and when she came after me I killed her, just as I had killed April. After that I carried her up to Neville's jeep. She was surprisingly light—or perhaps I was just so strong . . . When Marney left that evening I pretended to go after him—I'd already removed the papers to give me an excuse—but all I did was drive Neville's jeep with Melissa's body in it up to the plantation and dig that grave. Afterwards I went on to the lodge, dropped the papers through the letter-box, and drove home. I had to bury her on the plantation because the ground is so rocky and hard all around the house—it's impossible to dig a grave here without a lot of effort and trouble and I wanted so much to get rid of the body, bury it, forget about it—" She stopped. Harsh sobs shook her from head to toe; her face crumpled as she pressed her fingers against her eyes to try to obliterate the tears.

There was a deep horrified silence.

At last Neville said slowly: "I don't believe you, Leonie. You're making it up to protect us both."

She shook her head dumbly, her sobs muffled.

The silence fell again. And then into that silence Karen heard herself say calmly: "If you killed April, Leonie, you'll know where her grave is. Where is she buried?"

For a moment she thought Leonie wasn't going to answer. Then: "I shall tell the police," Leonie managed to say unevenly, "but I shan't tell any of you. I shall tell the police to prove to them that I killed her."

"They might still think you were covering up for one of us."

"No," said Leonie with a strange incisiveness. "I was the only person who could have buried April in this particular place. I shall explain to the police and they'll understand why."

"Then tell us."

She shook her head stubbornly. "No."

Neville's glance met Marney's. They looked at one another for a long moment. Then:

"In that case I suppose I'd better call the police, hadn't I," said Marney bleakly, and moved with bowed head out into the hall.

5

The police arrived from Fort William towards the end of the morning. Leonie had retired to her room as soon as Marney had made the telephone call, and on Neville's advice. Karen had also gone upstairs to rest for a while. When he and Marney were alone together Neville had telephoned the lodge, spoken to Kelleher to say he and Marney would be at the house until further notice, and had then had a word with Thomas. By the time Thomas himself arrived at the house, three quarters of an hour later after walking over the pass from the plantation, Snuff was up and Karen had returned downstairs to cook breakfast.

But except for the child no one was hungry.

The morning seemed interminable. At last Karen, her head aching with the tension, went to lie down again, and when she awoke later from a brief sleep it was almost noon and the police were downstairs in the living-room. She was just wondering whether she should join them when she heard Neville go into Leonie's room next door to summon her.

"Leonie . . ." She could hear his voice faintly through the wall, but then there was a long silence. After a minute or two of further silence she heard him leave the room and run quickly downstairs.

She got up, spurred on by an unreasoning sense of dread. She was just slipping on her robe when there were footsteps on the stairs again, and the next moment Neville came into the room.

He was very white.

"Neville—"

"I'm afraid Leonie's taken too many sleeping pills," he said unsteadily. "We've phoned for a doctor and one of the policemen is just trying artificial respiration."

"My God." Her mind was spinning dizzily, and as she sat down again on the edge of the bed she did not at first hear his next words.

"Karen—did you hear me?" He was leaning over her, his face taut and strained. "She left a confession, Karen, a written confession for the police. She told them where to find April's grave."

She stared up at him blankly. "Where is it? Where did she say it was?"

"Beneath the rock garden," said Neville. "The rock garden she was beginning when I brought April to the farm three years ago."

6

Leonie's note was more stark than Karen had expected. She had simply written:

To Whom It May Concern:

In the presence of my brother Neville Bennett, his wife Karen, and Dr. Marney West, I explained how I killed April Conway and Melissa Fleming. They also know why I killed each woman, and know that Melissa's grave is on the boundary of the plantation nearest to the house. April's grave is beneath the rock garden. No one else knows that except me, because no one else could have buried her there. I was beginning the rock garden when I arrived at the house for my holiday that year—I already had a pile of stones and small rocks assembled and I intended to spend my holiday arranging them and planting flowers. When I killed April my first thought was to hide the body before Neville came back to the house, so I took the body outside and piled the rocks and stones over it until it was completely hidden. Once that was done I packed her suitcases and took them to the only soft ground I knew, the floor of the ruined house. It wasn't until both suitcases were buried that I realized I wouldn't be able to bury the body there as I'd hoped—the rest of the floor was granite and there was no more room. I then towed the spare boat across the lake to make it look as if she had rowed herself across, but I didn't dare set about digging a grave for the body because I knew it would take a long time and I was frightened of being discovered before I had finished. I decided to leave the body where it was until I knew I would be alone for some hours. In the end, however, the opportunity to dig the grave arrived sooner than I had expected—Neville left Scotland that same day to follow Karen and Thomas back to London, and Marney, his business completed, went with him. Those are details that can

*be verified, and they're important because they prove that
neither Neville nor Marney had the chance to dig a proper
grave for the body. I did. I stayed on at the house and managed after much labor and effort to do what had to be
done. The ground was very hard and stony and I nearly
despaired of ever being able to go deep enough. This also
can be verified when the body is exhumed, and it will prove
that whoever dug the grave spent several hours digging it.
Finally when I had finished I piled the rocks and stones up
over the grave and spent a long time working on the rock
garden so that no one would ever suspect what lay beneath
it.*

*I have no more to add except that both women were
despicable creatures and if it were not for the fact that to
kill is evil and unchristian I would never regret that I had
caused their deaths.*

*Please conclude any public investigation as quietly as
possible for the sake of my nephew, who is as yet too young
to understand why I should feel my life is finished and why
I should thus seek to end it of my own accord.*

7

"I feel numb," said Karen slowly to Neville. "Numb
and upset and very tired. I feel as if I'm incapable of
making any decisions about what to do next."

He smiled. Strain and shock had made him look
suddenly older and less debonair, but despite his care-
worn looks his smile still held a trace of his old self.
"You needn't worry," he told her wryly, "because I've
already made your decisions for you." He put his arms
around her and stooped to give her a kiss. "After all
this is over, I shall take you on a cruise—perhaps a
Hellenic cruise to Greece. I know you always wanted
to go there, and cruises are the ideal way to travel—

we'll both get plenty of opportunity to rest and push Scotland to the back of our minds. Snuff can come with us—if you don't mind him coming—"

"Of course he must come! How could we go without him?"

He smiled at her again. "Then it's settled! We'll have a long holiday and then when we get back to London after the cruise I might consider leaving the British Isles for a while—I'll certainly sell the farm. I couldn't return here for a holiday again. As far as my work's concerned, I've had an excellent offer recently from some forestry people in Canada, a two-year assignment —" He saw Karen stiffen. She was by the window, looking out towards the burn. "What's the matter?"

She shook her head. "Nothing, just the police. They're starting their investigations of the rock garden."

8

They were already investigating at Plantation Q. The police inspector in charge believed in being thorough and taking nothing on trust, not even a convenient suicide note, and so even as Leonie's rock garden was carefully dismantled, the area around Melissa's grave was being subjected to close scrutiny. The police worked methodically and patiently, and then just as they were debating whether to explore deeper in the woods, a jeep arrived from the house with word that the body of a young woman had been uncovered beneath the rock garden which Leonie had tended for so long with such loving care.